Two Sides To Every Story

Women Like Us, Volume 3

Brenda K. Stone

Published by Brenda K. Stone, 2018.

TWO SIDES TO EVERY STORY

First edition. December 17, 2018.

Written by Brenda K. Stone.

Dedication

This book is dedicated to my guardian angels: my beloved father and mother, Albert and Jennie, and my sister Margo.

This book is also dedicated to my sisters Marie and Jeanne, and my niece Amanda.

Acknowledgements

Thank you to my sister Marie for reading my books, even though the *New York Times* is much more your thing.

Thank you also to my friend and fellow author Judy Kentrus, for all the guidance you've given me, even when you had your own work to do and your own problems to overcome.

The Witch

NO WOMAN WANTS TO HEAR the words Bob spoke to me after fifteen year of marriage and four beautiful daughters.

"Carla, I have something to tell you."

He had not given me even the slightest warning. Not that we had the greatest marriage, not that we were blissfully happy, but we loved each other, or so I thought, and we did anything for our girls that we had to do to keep our home and our family secure.

"What is it, Bob? Is everything okay?" Of course, I was worried. Bob was rarely as serious as he was then.

"Carla, I've found someone new, and I'm in love with her. I want a divorce."

"What—? How—?" Too many questions were jammed in my head, but only a couple of words managed to escape. Thank goodness the girls had not come home from school yet. I wouldn't have wanted them to see me like that.

Bob, on the other side of the kitchen table, simply shook his head at me and said flatly, "Never mind what and how. It happened because it had to happen, because I wanted it to happen."

"Had to happen? Wanted it to happen?" The incomprehensible words gushed out now.

Coldly, Bob spit, "Carla, don't act like you don't know what I mean."

"I don't know what you mean! Bob...?"

"I'm leaving."

And, bag already packed, he did. Without another word, without saying good-bye to the girls. Into the arms of the Homewrecker.

The hell had only just begun.

The Homewrecker

OCCASIONALLY, THE MEMORIES come flooding back, even now.

"Bob, am I a homewrecker?" I had begged to know, tears of uncertainty streaking my cheeks.

"No, baby, Carla wrecked her own home. Wrecked me, wrecked her daughters. They like you more than her," he'd assured me.

"Thank you." How I'd clung to his words, and to him!

"I never knew I could be this happy," Bob had cried that night. "Fifteen years of hating my life everyday..." I'd never seen a grown man shed tears the way he did.

"Baby, that's all over now. We're starting a new life together," I reminded him.

"By the time she gets everything she wants there's going to be nothing left to me," he warned, and not for the first time.

"As long as we have each other, that's all that matters." My response was not new, either. It was worth repeating. He had to know I meant it.

"Molly, I'll never forget the first time I saw you. I knew my whole life was going to change," Bob whispered.

I knew, too, but I didn't know how it would happen, how long it would take.

A year and a half had gone by since we'd met at the restaurant I managed. Bob came to me a wounded man. I made him feel comfortable, like he could trust me. He kept coming back. And slowly, he opened up to me. We became casual friends first. Time worked its magic. It was meant to be.

"We did it, Bob," I said, with a soft laugh.

"Yeah. Here's to our next fifteen years without her around." Bob chuckled, too.

And then we kissed.

"Homewrecker?" Bob had sniffed. "Hardly. The witch should be thanking you. You've saved her family from hating her."

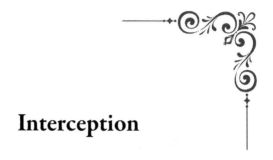

Interception

Carla

BOB IS A WELL-KNOWN man in our small city. He's one of only three certified public accountants in Farmingdale, and he was the busiest and most trusted of the three. Bob knows the financial secrets of everyone and took care of the monetary affairs of anyone who matters in town, as well as many who don't, but hope to. He was popular and had a spotless reputation. Christmas gifts came from satisfied customers, thank you cards loaded his business mailbox every year after April fifteenth. Even free football tickets appeared magically, because Bob made it very well known that he's a super fan.

Maybe I should have been cautious. Women had always been interested in my handsome and knowledgeable husband.

Well, ex-husband now. That title is still a bitter pill to have to swallow. Especially after all the promises, assurances.

"Carla, you never have to worry about us. Getting rid of me is going to be pretty hard!" he'd joke.

Bob was so proud of the life he built for us and our four daughters. Built it from scratch, from the ground up. We were high school sweethearts who literally started out with nothing but the shoes on our feet, and even those weren't in very good shape. Bob's parents were absent most of his life, mine were workaholics. Both of us were mostly raised by caring family members, Bob by his paternal grandmother, me by my mother's younger sister. He and I were a needy pair, and we fulfilled each other. We were married the day after high school graduation, much to the chagrin of our families. Our first daughter, Becky, was three months in the womb when Bob was hardly out of his third string quarterback uniform.

"I want a big family, Carla. To make up for being an only child," Bob had murmured to me on our wedding night. We were well on our way to creating that.

"We'll have an amazing family," I promised. My body was a small sacrifice to make for Bob's happiness.

Bob hated being an only child and growing up lonely. He was and is a "people person." Back then, he wanted to change his life in every way, and did. He made it what he wanted it to be, and all along I thought I was a major part of it. It's so comforting to believe you're part of someone's dream, and devastating to find out that you really aren't.

The babies came so quickly, maybe we never had time to work on our relationship. At the time, it felt like everything was falling into place for us. Pictures of Bob cradling Becky, our first baby, seem to echo that belief, even now. We all suddenly had each other, and life was so comfortable and meaningful. Everything was different, better, for both of us.

While Bob went to night school to be an accountant I stayed home with the girls as they came one after the other, four daughters in eight years. By the time we were both twenty-five Becky, Jenna, Emily, and Amy had already been born. Our family was complete!

Bob worked a lot, I watched a lot of soap operas and dreamed the dreams of a housewife while I cleaned the house and cooked fantastic meals. I never questioned our happiness. We seemed to be the typical American family. Big, beautiful house, children involved in sports, music, and lasting friendships, two shining cars in the garage. We went on weekend camping trips, Disney vacations in the summer, the ever-present football games. Bob and I had like-minded friends. Twice a year, when Bob could tear himself away from his accounting office, we'd go on romantic getaways together.

"I never thought we would have all this, Carla. Life is so good," he said to me on our fourteenth anniversary, at an all-inclusive resort in Aruba.

He already knew the woman I came to call the Homewrecker. I still search for signs I should have caught in Aruba. They had to have been there, staring me in the face! Less than a year later my life, and the lives of our daughters, was devastated.

When I search the evidence, I can only come up with one thing, and that was how our kids started to relate to us. The girls, Becky, Jenna, Emily, and Amy, teenagers or on their way there, had started to run to Bob when I would say no to something. Becky and Jenna, the two oldest, were especially obvious.

"Dad, tell Mom that it's not that big of a deal!" one of them would protest, when I might be on edge about letting them attend a pool party at the house of a friend when we didn't know the parents, or going out after dark to a movie where boys their age or older would be present.

"Carla, let's just give her a chance to do the right thing," Bob, the easy-going one, might say to me. And I would relent, chocking it up to a "female thing" between the girls and me.

Teenage girls aren't exactly easy to deal with. Add to that the real fact that I was barely in my mid-thirties and never did anything like that when I was their age, and maybe some would say that it was a recipe for disaster.

And then there was *her.* Molly.

She worked at a mid-priced chain restaurant at the local mall, surrounded on all sides by trendy shops that teens like to hang around in. The girls said she was a "manager," but my observation at the time was that she was nothing more than a two-bit waitress. Bob and I met all four girls there on a Sunday afternoon when we let them roam free for a couple of hours with a gaggle of their friends. The late spring weekend was coming to a close, and we would end it with a family dinner. Electricity and anticipation were already in the air with the school year commencing in two weeks and a family cruise to the Caribbean planned. And then, along came Molly to heighten the bliss. Molly, with her shiny, straight brown hair, natural smile, and alarming green eyes.

"That lady is so nice, and pretty, too. We see her all the time when we come here with our friends," Jenna crooned, as Molly took an order at a table close by. "She gives us extra fries."

I remember feeling jealous then, with my girls mooning over this stranger who had already won their affections through, of all things, French fries! After Bob left me I had to stop my mind from thinking that Molly had plotted the demise of my marriage and family life through the junk food choices of several hungry teenagers. Minds do strange things when they're in shock.

"Hey girls, how are you doing today?" Molly bubbled when she came over to us. "Drinking the usual pitcher of orange soda?"

My legs were sweating and sticking to the vinyl cushion on the dark wood chair as four looks of love appeared on the faces of my girls. I shifted uneasily, hoping my skin peeling away from the pillow wouldn't make an embarrassing sound.

Bob smiled up at Molly, who had a black nametag pinned onto her starched white blouse.

"I hear you're good for free fries?" he teased easily.

I slipped my hand into the crook of his arm.

"Shh, don't blow my cover!" Molly joked. She seemed so natural. "Are these your lovely daughters?" The question was directed at Bob, and I felt slighted that she didn't even move her eyes in my direction.

"Yes, these are our girls," I answered.

When Bob wiggled his arm under my hand, I realized that I was clutching him.

"They're so nice and well behaved. Best kids that come in here. Always polite, and they set excellent examples for their friends."

Even though Molly was handing out a great compliment I was offended. How could she claim to know anything about my children from seeing them in a restaurant a few times?

"Thanks, Molly. We know we have great kids, but it's nice to hear it from other people," Bob offered.

Molly continued some banter about orange soda and seasoned fries with the girls, then bounced off. Bob definitely watched her for a moment. I'm certain of that. Or, am I just making an assumption after the fact?

"She was pleasant," he commented. "Not too often you meet a happy waitress."

When Molly came back with our drinks, I searched her hand for a wedding band, or at least a diamond, finding nothing. Before long I let go of my envy and felt much more comfortable with the family conversation that ensued. But I filed it in a small drawer in my mind that Bob and I wouldn't make a habit of meeting our girls at this particular restaurant.

Molly

CARLA SEEMED LIKE SUCH a drama queen. Bob said it wasn't at all like she told it. He had poor self-esteem as a teenager because of his crappy family life. His precise words to me were, "I didn't think I could get anyone better than Carla. I'm totally guilty of taking the first thing that came along. I had to escape my family. I was so young!"

As a single woman who has never wanted children, I knew I was taking on a lot by getting involved with Bob. I never saw myself with a man with four kids, but Bob was everything I could have asked for in a partner, and I loved the kids, too. Just like I told Bob and Carla when I first met them, the girls were great. Smart, kind, attractive.

"They got all the good stuff from you," I teased Bob.

"Well, maybe we should give Carla a little bit of credit," he said sheepishly.

"If you say so, Bob!" I rolled my eyes.

I knew he was just trying to be nice. He didn't do that too often.

It was more like him to call his ex a lunatic. "She even looks like one. I swear she hasn't gotten a haircut in twenty years, and her clothes are atrocious. She doesn't have an ounce of fashion sense," he griped.

She was so nondescript, I didn't even remember what she looked like the one time I met her.

"Well, I'm not exactly a trend setter!" I pointed out.

"You're so pretty, Molly. I'm a lucky, lucky man," Bob insisted.

Comments like these lessened the burden of being the new woman in Bob's life.

One of the worst days of our relationship was when Carla called my cell and started ranting at me, "You stole my husband out from underneath me, you homewrecker! Everything was fine until you came along and screwed up our lives!" I didn't know how she got my phone number until Bob's youngest girl, Amy, confessed that her mother had tricked her into giving it to her before Amy attended a football game with Bob and I.

"Mom said that she wouldn't use it, just needed it in case there were any emergencies while I was at the game with you and Daddy," Amy murmured.

I couldn't imagine messing with the mind of a nine-year-old like that. No wonder the kids didn't want to go home, no wonder they wanted Bob and me to buy a house together, so they didn't have to go back to her.

That night, after all the girls were asleep in my spare room, I asked him again, "Bob, everything wasn't fine, right?"

Before I even finished my sentence, he was shaking his head, holding my shoulders. "No, Molly. You know the truth. Don't let her get into your mind. She's good at that. She's been messing with mine for years." To lighten the mood Bob kissed my lips softly and said, "Besides, she didn't even know what a first down is!"

We cracked up laughing, a tense conversation diverted that easily. My fondness for football was a cause for celebration between us.

When Bob and Carla first came to the restaurant with their girls, I knew they weren't happy, and it had nothing to do with a game where grown men throw a pigskin around. I saw how she hung on his arm and recognized her envy. She appeared a lot older than Bob, and was rude to me when I said anything, even though I was just doing my job.

Did I feel something for Bob that very first day I met him? I thought he was very friendly and handsome, and I knew his name because the general manager of the restaurant used Bob as his accountant. But I had no motive to pursue him. A homewrecker I wasn't. But at the time I was the manager of the dining room staff, in addition to being a waitress. That part is accurate.

I saw the girls two more times after that before Bob showed up at the restaurant's bar one day by himself. He smiled and waved at me, and I was taken aback by the sadness in his posture. Nevertheless, I approached him to say hello, remembering his face because I was so fond of the four girls.

"Aren't you the French fry lady?" he kidded.

"Are they still spreading rumors about me?" I said with a chuckle.

"They talk about you a lot!" he admitted.

Not that I know a lot about kids, but all I could think was that if Bob's girls were talking so much about me, something must be wrong at home.

"All good, of course," I kept the light mood going.

"Good? No, great! My daughters rarely talk about any grown-up like that. You've made quite an impression on them."

The restaurant was starting to fill up. One of my fellow waitresses limped by bearing a heavy tray laden with food. "Table 35 is complaining that no one is taking their order," she informed me, with a motion of her head toward the open dining area.

"I just took their drink orders and am getting them now," I replied, with a roll of my eyes.

"Well, you know how some of them get." I barely heard Tanya, because she was moving away from me.

I turned back to Bob. "I'd better get back to work here before I get denied a tip."

"Thanks for stopping by. It was really nice to see you again." Bob's tone wasn't one of a married family man, nor was the twinkle in his eyes as he met mine. Believe me, I was already confused.

"Same here. Tell the girls I said hello," I said softly, feeling a pang of interest in the core of my stomach.

"Will do."

Bob spent a good hour and a half at the bar. His gaze followed me on my frequent trips to the kitchen.

"Who's the guy?" Tanya asked, as we were both picking up orders.

"Which one?" I knew who she was talking about, but I was curious about her impression of Bob. Tanya had been a waitress for twenty-five years and had seen just about everything.

"The good-looking one at the bar that can't seem to take his eyes off you," she teased.

So, it wasn't my imagination. If Tanya saw it, too, there must have been some basis to my observations.

"Oh, he's the father of some nice young ladies that come in here a lot when they're hanging around the mall with their friends," I said casually.

"Divorced?" Tanya must have been lobbying to get me a date. She knew I'd broken up with a guy a few months before and had been lonely since.

"I'm not sure," I admitted, and I wasn't.

Bob and Carla had been in the restaurant together three months before, so I had to assume they were still a couple. The girls had not indicated anything wrong at home, either.

"Maybe you should find out." Tanya took her order from the cook and walked off, throwing a smile over her shoulder at me.

I laughed, but when I walked by the bar again to deliver my order Bob was gone. Guess I wasn't going to find out that day.

"He's back," Tanya whispered to me a week later, nodding toward the bar.

I tipped my head to look around a partition and saw Bob nursing a draft beer, staring down at the drink, fidgeting with a small napkin.

I grinned at Tanya, trying not to let any emotions show. Had I been thinking about Bob? Yes, I was guilty. But I had to be careful with my heart. The guy who I had just ended a relationship with had been cheating on me, and there was no way I was getting into another situation like that. Having anything to do with a married man was an accident waiting to happen.

My feet didn't get the message. I made it a point to walk by him, and he brightened right away.

"Hi, Molly! Seeing you is just what I needed today. I feel better already."

"Tough day?" I asked.

"Really tough. And I don't want to go home, because things are only going to get worse." He shook his head, dropped his eyes again.

"I'm sorry about that. Did you have a fight with your wife?" I hoped I didn't sound obvious, but this was my chance to find out why Bob was showing up at the restaurant.

He shook his head. "No, I'm just not happy at home. Never was, guess I never will be."

I noticed that hardly any of the beer was gone.

"When I saw you with your family you all looked so—" I grasped for a word, suddenly remembering the way his wife had been holding tightly to his arm. "Content," I finally blurted, the first thing that popped into my head.

Bob shrugged, appearing pained. "Thank you. I guess we're putting up a pretty good façade."

The restaurant was quiet that afternoon, and I only had an hour before my shift ended.

"Well, whatever it is, I hope you're able to work it out." I was at a total loss for words after this, so I just smiled softly and started to move away.

"Listen Molly, would you like to sit down and talk one of these days? Maybe over a coffee? I promise I won't just complain about my problems." Bob seemed desperate to keep me there.

I swallowed hard. "I'm not sure how to answer. I mean, are you getting a divorce?"

Bob frowned and lifted his brows. "I'm afraid to ask for one. Carla will take everything I've worked so hard for over the past fifteen years. And she'll take my girls, too." He pushed the beer aside and stood up. "I understand how you feel. I guess I wouldn't get involved with me, either. Listen, thanks for being so nice to my daughters."

He started to shuffle away.

I panicked.

One word fell from my lips: "Wait!"

When Bob turned back to me, I knew I was committed.

Carla

I KNOW THIS IS A FOOLISH thing to bring up, or to think it had anything to do with the demise of our relationship, but Bob is incredibly serious about football. I'd go as far as to say that he's a fanatic, and he wanted me to be one, too.

The game was his first love in high school, and he was always jealous of the boys who got to play all the time, while he warmed the bench. He never wanted to believe that the coach took mercy on him and gave him a uniform just because the fatherly man knew what kind of life Bob had, but I knew the truth. Coach Gallagher was a notorious softie and had even taken in a couple of boys that were promising athletes.

"Coach might let me play tomorrow night," was a popular refrain from Bob. The few times it happened were disasters, but Bob didn't give up easily. At least not until he got a knee injury that blessedly ended his football career forever at the tender age of seventeen. Bob still has the slightest limp because of it, but I think the real damage was to his ego. Choosing to become an accountant was always second best, but he eventually came to accept it, and was very successful at it.

"We have to have a boy, so he can become a star quarterback," he would say all three times I became pregnant after the birth of our first daughter. Whether we're together or not, I'll always give Bob credit for loving our kids, though I think that every time I failed to give him a boy, he was just a little put off that he didn't get his future quarterback.

As for me, I tried to be a part of his love for the game, but I think he knew that it wasn't for me. When we were in high school, I'd worry about him constantly, and resented his place on the team, even while I knew it would never come to anything. Later, when he tried to teach me the basics of the game, so I would know what was going on when we attended one, I just couldn't, or maybe didn't want to, grasp it.

"The team has four tries to make a first down, but usually punts on the fourth down," Bob tried to explain. "It's ten yards for a first down."

"What is a down?" I asked, exasperated because the game, though definitely exciting and emotional, just didn't make sense to me. No matter what, all I saw was a pile of bodies belonging to grown men. At one time, my beloved husband, the only man I had ever been with, had been one of those dirty guys grunting over a ball that was quite small compared to them.

"Never mind. You'll figure it out. Just keep watching."

I kept watching but didn't figure it out. It hardly mattered, because one by one our girls became fans and watched the games with their father. In the fall, when the weather was getting cooler and the girls had school work to contend with, Sunday afternoons became nice family times. I'd be in the room, too, but might be knitting or flipping through a women's magazine while they cheered for the home team.

"Thank goodness someone gets it!" Bob huffed one afternoon, directing a cold look at me.

I thought he was kidding. After all, football is only a game. Maybe it did matter in the end.

Bob had always worked long hours, but the last few months of our marriage they got even longer. I know now that he wasn't at the office but was planning a new life for himself behind my back. Visiting the Homewrecker at the restaurant, telling her lies about me, turning my daughters against me.

The girls already had a head start. At fifteen, thirteen, eleven, and nine, and with all the trimmings of modern kids—the phones, the clothes, the popularity at school—their attitudes were enormous. Emily and Amy, the two younger ones, were taking notes from Becky and Jenna, their bossy older sisters.

"I'll get my homework done tomorrow on the bus. It's so easy, Mom!" Becky might complain. "Can you give me a ride to Ava's house?"

I was running the show myself, because sometimes I couldn't even get in touch with Bob on his cell. His secretary only worked until three, so he didn't answer the office phone after she left. The cell was the only option. Never guessing what he was really up to, I'd try once, give up, and have to deal with the girls myself.

"No, just do your homework and you can see Ava over the weekend." My demand would be met by teenager protests.

"I'm calling Dad!" Becky might shriek.

Bob often answered their calls when I couldn't get through to him on my cell. I think he picked and chose. But it was almost inevitable that whatever phone made the connection with him would be thrust at me in anger.

"Dad wants to talk to you!"

"Carla, I told Becky to listen to what you told her. But I can't see why she shouldn't go to Ava's house. We see the homework she gets, and it's too easy for her. She isn't lying when she says she can do it on the bus." Bob always tried to make disagreeing with me as painless as possible. Now I know why.

During this particular conflict, I remember hearing glasses clinking in the background and the faint sounds of a television set, even though Bob was supposed to be "working late," and I knew he didn't have a TV in his office. One of the many things I tried to pass off as "my imagination." The more I think, the more I realize there were so many signs that I was missing, that I really didn't want to see.

"Bob, I'm here, you're there," I reminded him.

"You're right, Carla. And I trust you to make the right decision." Bob gave in easily. He obviously had other concerns.

Our daughters didn't give in nearly as simply as he did and fought me tooth and nail on anything that didn't go their way. They would gang up against me, their own mother! Bob would always smooth it over when he got home. But the resentment was building.

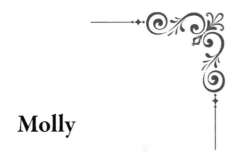

Molly

"THE GIRLS ARE SO FED up with her. All day, all I get is calls from them. 'Mom won't let me do this, Mom won't let me do that.' I'm sick of it, Molly! I don't know what's wrong with her."

Even though Bob said he wouldn't talk about his troubles the whole time, when we first started to get together, he just seemed so wounded that I let him get off his chest whatever he needed to. I hardly talked about my own problems and worries.

"It must be hard to be so young and have so many kids. Especially all girls!" I didn't know Carla other than the one time she had come to the restaurant, and I felt like I had to stick up for my fellow woman, put myself in her shoes. Four kids, and we were almost the same age. I was just three years younger and had none!

"She was the one that wanted all the kids, not me. We didn't use birth control, and she just kept getting pregnant."

"You didn't want..." My voice drifted off, and I felt awful, because I was so fond of the girls. He must have seen something in my expression, because he was quick to defend his kids.

"I didn't mean that the way it sounded, Molly. They mean the world to me and I don't regret having them. It's just that Carla got me into so many things I didn't want to be in. I wanted to play football professionally but ended up an accountant instead to feed my family."

"Really, Bob? That's so interesting."

Bob didn't elaborate, even though I was hoping he would. I made a mental note to find out more about his football dream another time.

The first couple of times we got together I chose to do it in the restaurant, with people I knew around. Even though Bob was a familiar figure in town I didn't completely trust him at first. Then again, I probably wouldn't have trusted any other man, either, given some of the relationships I'd had. Sometimes people he knew would come in, so we sat at a table for two toward the back of the dining room where there were more shadows than light. He also made sure that his kids wouldn't be in the mall the days we met.

"They like you a lot, but I don't know how they would react if they saw us together," he explained.

"I don't think it's a good idea they see us together," I murmured, wondering for the millionth time already if I was doing the right thing by getting to know Bob.

"So, I guess I don't have any kind of chance with you, huh?" he asked, not meeting my eyes.

Bob had a way of avoiding eye contact when he was saying something important. And this was pretty big, because up until now I wasn't completely sure that Bob wanted "a chance" with me. Maybe he just wanted someone to talk to. I'd been through that, too.

I shrugged and said, "I'm not sure, Bob. I mean, I think you're great. But you haven't really told me what you're planning to do with your life. Until I know that I'm not going to get too close, because I don't want to be hurt, either."

Bob nodded with a look of understanding. "I wouldn't want to hurt you. And to tell you the truth, Molly, I don't know what I'm going to do. But if I decided to leave Carla would you date me?" From across the table his hand crept toward mine, and he rubbed my knuckles. "I think you're great, too."

"I would date you, Bob. But it would have to be over between you and your wife," I replied with total sincerity.

"Of course. I'm pretty sure it's over for me, but that doesn't mean I can just leave her. There's a lot at stake."

Too much must have been a stake, because Bob disappeared for several weeks after that. However, I saw the girls. They came into the restaurant and acted differently than usual. The two oldest ones, Becky and Jenna, were with boys that were considerably older than them, and they were loud and silly. I still gave them extra fries and gleaned some upsetting but interesting information from overhearing some adolescent banter from one of the young men present.

"I wish your mom and dad went to Aruba every week!"

"Believe me, so do I!" Becky, the oldest girl, agreed with her cute date.

My heart thumped in my chest, tears rushed to my eyes. My feet felt like I was walking in wet concrete.

"Hey Molly, are you okay?" Tanya called as I made a break for the ladies room.

I couldn't turn to answer because I didn't want her to see my tears.

Bob had evidently made his choice. It was back to the drawing board for me.

In true fashion of the dreaded "other woman," something I had no interest in being, it wasn't until I knew that Bob was frolicking in an island paradise with the mother of his children that I realized I was madly in love with him.

Carla

MOLLY GOT IT RIGHT. Aruba *was* paradise, even if things at home between me and my daughters were starting to crumble.

"Bob, I just feel like the girls are getting away from me," I had sobbed to him as soon as we were relaxed, unpacked, and had shaken off our jet lag.

"Oh hell, Carla, Becky and Jenna are teenagers, and Amy and Emily are almost there. Don't you think it's perfectly natural that they're trying to defy you?" Bob tried to comfort me.

"Maybe you're right. But—"

"Honey, it's just you and me. How much time do we have like this? Let's just love it while we're here and worry about the girls when we get back. We'll just work harder as a family, okay? Everything will be alright. Let's live it up!"

And we did. It was like we were teenagers again. We reveled in each other, and the life we had built together.

"We have it all, Carla," Bob moaned, after we made sweet and tender love, something we seemed to take less and less time to do.

I held him to me and whispered, "We're so lucky."

The girls stayed with a young woman in town that was a professional babysitter. She wasn't much older than Becky, so it shouldn't have been a big surprise to find out that she had let them have boyfriends over, and they had not done their homework the whole time we were gone. Needless to say, she was unceremoniously fired, and the girls were grounded for a week when we returned home.

"Oh my god, Mom, I can't believe how much I hate you!" Becky had screamed, slamming the door of her room in my face, after I told her she wouldn't be allowed to see her friends until the following weekend.

That word jarred me. *Hate.*

"And you need to break up with that boy. He's too old for you," I pushed.

"I love Evan, and I'm not breaking up with him. You can go to hell!"

Everything good that had happened in Aruba seemed to shatter that quickly with a few ugly words from my fifteen-year-old daughter. Little did I know that a waitress at a restaurant in the mall saw my girls with their boyfriends and knew more about them than their own mother.

"Now what?" I sobbed to my husband.

And he soothed me, "Just let things cool down, and everything will be okay."

Bob sure seemed to be dead set on everything being okay. Yet, life as I knew it was crumbling faster than the Great Sphinx of Giza.

I couldn't let it go. My daughter telling me she hated me, and that I could go to hell.

"I want an apology," I told Bob the following morning, even though he wanted me to "chill out."

"Carla—" Bob was in our bathroom shaving before he went to work, and he met my eyes in the mirror. I knew he was going to protest, so I got my twenty-five cents in while he was still concentrating on not cutting his face to shreds.

"What she said to me is not acceptable. We need to sit down with her before she goes to school. I'll drive her in late, so we can get this out of the way."

Bob swung his eyes away from me, not confirming or disagreeing. I stomped back into the bedroom to throw the bed together before I dressed.

Bob's wallet was on the bedside table, and a small white rectangle of paper was sticking out of it. Glancing at it with little interest, I saw that it was a receipt of some kind. Printed at the top was the name and address of the restaurant in the mall where the girls got their free fries from "Molly." Molly of the shimmering hair and green eyes. The woman I would nickname the Homewrecker.

After Becky had treated me so badly the night before, and the younger girls hadn't done me any favors, either, Bob had left the house, saying he was going to the office to check up on what had accumulated in his absence. I didn't give it more than a passing thought. *Must be an old receipt,* I'd mused. *Or maybe something the girls gave him?* And I'd finished making the bed we had just shared. We had not made love that evening after Becky's outburst, after he'd arrived home close to midnight from the "office," but had done our usual cuddling. Maybe it was a little less close? Maybe he was colder than usual? Later I would wonder, was he with her the evening before? Did he shower when he got home to get rid of the scent of her? Or maybe he was at her home and had showered there, before driving home and crawling into bed with me? Highly unproductive thoughts that only hurt me more. But after being left in the lurch by a man I thought I knew for fifteen years who suddenly had nothing to say to me, it was only natural that I'd still try to wrap my mind around all of it.

That morning I dressed quickly after making the bed and waited patiently for Bob to come out of the bathroom. He seemed to be disappointed to find me on the edge of the bed, but I wasn't backing down on getting an apology from our eldest.

"Just let me get dressed, then we'll talk to her," he said softly.

Bob was shirtless but had put expensive jeans on. I admired his thin, strong chest and back, his dark, curly hair. For the umpteeth time I considered Bob's status in town, his appealing appearance, the dollar amounts on his bank accounts and retirement funds. I was certainly a fortunate woman to have such a man, but Bob never made a big deal about it. Our differences were a moot point with him. How many times had I heard, *Carla, you're perfect just the way you are?* And, *you're everything I want and more?*

And yet, I caught a passing glimpse of my reflection in the full-length mirror on the bedroom door across the room and felt like I had never looked at myself. Maybe I didn't; maybe I didn't want to see Carla, because perhaps I didn't like her. What I saw was a frumpy thirty-three-year-old with drab hair and a few extra pounds. A woman who had dedicated her life to her family and had always felt good about it, but now that her work was showing signs of wear and tear, a woman who needed more out of life and knew how many changes she would have to make to get it. Maybe her husband wouldn't even want her to change, even if she wanted to.

My most crushing thought of all was, *Are my girls and my husband ashamed of me?*

A mid-life crisis too soon.

"Hey, isn't it about time to get your hair done?" Bob inquired, for the first time ever, pulling me out of my daze.

He had a sleek black button-down shirt tucked into his jeans, with an expensive leather belt pulling the look together.

"Yes, Bob. I'll make an appointment," I answered mechanically, feeling like the beast to his beauty.

"Well, let's go talk to Becky," he urged.

I was so down on myself that he had to remind me what I was doing there.

All the signs were laid out in front of me and I didn't see them.

Molly

"HOW WAS ARUBA?" I TRIED to sound spiteful, but my voice came out too friendly. I was so happy to see him.

"How did you know I was in Aruba?" Bob couldn't hide his surprise.

"Your kids were in here while you were gone, and I over-heard a little of their conversation." I didn't want to incriminate the girls for my own benefit. They already had enough problems.

"To answer your question, it wasn't so great, Molly. I guess I thought of the trip as a last-ditch effort to save our marriage, and, well, it didn't work."

Any scheme I had to be upset with Bob ended abruptly. I wanted to hear the magic word: *divorce.*

"I'm sorry, Bob." I was suddenly deeply ashamed of myself for thinking I had any claim on him and his time.

"I would have much rather spent the time with you," he admitted.

"I missed seeing you all this time," I murmured.

"Not as much as I missed you." Bob looked tired but hand-some, with his incredible grey eyes, long lashes, dark, pointed brows.

32

We were at our special table for the first time in two months, but I wanted to be somewhere, anywhere, out from under the gazes of my coworkers. I trusted Bob now.

"Do you want to come to my condo?" I asked boldly. "I just want to relax."

His chest rose and fell, a pleasant color heating his cheeks. "Molly, I'd love that."

My friend Tanya always kept a close eye on us, and usually I appreciated it. Tonight, I wanted to slip out from under her watch. "Why don't you go first, and I'll meet you out in the parking lot in a few minutes," I suggested.

"Sure, that's perfect." Bob couldn't keep a secret smile from turning up the corners of his lips.

Before long he was following me to my condo in a silver Infinity that must have set him back a pretty penny. It was one of the many reminders that I was starting a relationship with a man that was in deep with another woman.

I didn't care.

Knowing that Bob and Carla had one of the biggest houses in the finest part of town, I worried that Bob would come to my simple but clean and pretty condo and feel like he had just entered a slum. Just the opposite happened.

"Great place, Molly. So comfortable and happy," Bob commented, as I gave him the "grand tour" of the five rooms I called home.

I liked reproductions of famous paintings, particularly by Monet, and my furniture and curios had a decidedly floral theme. Bob's description was what I had been aiming for when I did my own designing of the place I had purchased two years before.

"I'm sure you're used to something a lot more fabulous," I said, my throat tight with nerves. I didn't want to disappoint him, because he seemed so far adrift already.

We made our way back to the living room and I motioned for him to relax on the couch.

As I settled down beside him Bob shrugged and replied, "Having a big house and fancy cars isn't everything, Molly. I've had all that for fifteen years and it's getting old. Carla doesn't work, so I'm forced to make enough to support us all. I'm at the office fifteen hours a day to pay for everything."

All my life I had worked for what I wanted. That's the way I was brought up, and I'd never really wanted it any other way. Maybe Carla didn't how to take care of herself. I had friends like that, and I didn't admire them. Because eventually...

"Did you ever ask her to get a job, so she could help you out?" I asked cautiously.

"Carla doesn't really have any skills, so whatever kind of job she got wouldn't help much, anyway." Bob sighed and continued, "Are you sure you want to get involved with the likes of me?"

I chuckled. "Bob, when you're in love with someone you take the good with the bad." My eyes saw a man that had more to offer me than I'd ever had in a lover.

"You're in love with me?" he asked, incredulously.

"Yes," I admitted, after taking a deep breath.

Bob reached out to cup my face in his hands. "Can I kiss you?" he whispered.

I nodded, but didn't speak, and his kiss came. Not a simple brush of my lips, but a passionate one, warm and breathy and long. When he let me up for air all I could say was, "Wow!"

"You took the words right out of my mouth," he said, laughing.

As I rose and took his hand to gently pull him off the couch, I was fully aware that he had just landed that morning from a vacation with his wife. Had they made love in Aruba? From the way he had described the trip as a "last ditch effort" to save their relationship, I imagined that either they hadn't, or that sex was so routine at that point that he derived no pleasure from it.

I didn't care either way. Because I would be sure that what we had together that night would erase all that for him and give him something to fantasize about during those fifteen-hour days in his accounting office.

Carla

WHAT MOLLY FAILED TO take into account was that Bob still had to be in that office to pay for all the toys we had, and to feed his family. For us: cars, boats, jet skis, timeshares, country club memberships. Mostly things that he wanted. For the girls: sports equipment, musical instruments and lessons, the latest fashions in the mall displays. Bills came in on a daily basis for all the things we owned but didn't really own. At least until I noticed something rather odd over the next few months: a lot of the daily mail we used to get stopped coming.

"I decided to set up online accounts, Carla," Bob explained, and me, the dutiful wife, didn't question it, even though it came as a surprise to me because Bob always said he liked things on paper. I know now that those bills were diverted for a much different reason, but at the time I took his word as gospel and kept cooking and cleaning for a husband and family that was becoming increasingly scarce. In fact, sometimes my meals went to waste and I had to try to salvage all my hard work by packing them up as school and work lunches.

One day, as my best friend Pam watched me taking a stack of plastic containers from a cabinet, she tried to convince me that Bob was likely engaging in "extra-curricular activities."

"Carla, the signs are all there. Jim was acting the same way before I found out about Kinky Boots."

I couldn't help but laugh ironically over Pam's moniker for the young assistant her husband had been having a secret affair with a few years back. Pam had chosen to forgive him, and they were doing well again. But I couldn't believe that Bob was following in Jim's footsteps. Jim had always seemed like a cheater to me, eyes wandering constantly, so I wasn't shocked to find out about "Kinky Boots." Bob, on the other hand, was so much more noble than that.

Wasn't he?

Partaking in the dreary task of separating turkey, gravy, and mashed potatoes into meal-sized portions in the containers, I shook my head in dispute. "Pam, Bob and I are fine. We're just in one of those valleys right now that everyone goes through. You know how many chances Bob has had to cheat, and he never has."

"That doesn't mean he won't, Carla," she pointed out.

I continued to dismiss Pam, feeling hurt and angry at her for even suggesting such an atrocity. Pam's accusation reinforced the feeling I'd always had that she had a little "thing" for my husband and was envious of our relationship.

Bob left early in the morning every day and didn't arrive back until at least seven at night, sometimes later. This was always the norm during tax season, so I wasn't suspicious. February was always a big month for him.

"More new customers, Carla. They're paying me well, so might as well enjoy it," he said at dinner one Friday night when we were all present, which didn't happen very often anymore.

Becky, Jenna, Emily, and Amy were quietly munching their food, completely uninterested in family time.

"Bob, you've always had new customers, and they never took this much time," I commented, Pam's words swirling through my head.

Jenna rolled her thirteen-year-old eyeballs. "Mom, why do you complain all the time? Can't you be happy about anything?" she demanded.

"Jenna, that's enough," Bob said quietly, his jaws working overtime as he chewed the prime rib I'd prepared just for him.

"This meat kind of sucks," Becky blurted, putting her fork down on her plate with a clank that echoed in the quiet dining room.

I put mine down, too, and dabbed at my mouth with a napkin before standing up slowly.

"I'm not quite sure why my family is treating me like this after all I've done for you, but if you can do better, please be my guest," I said, my chin up. Then I left the room. It was the first time I'd ever defended myself, and it was such a hard thing for me to do.

Later, after sulking in the master bedroom hoping Bob would at least come up and talk to me, I dragged down the stairs to find a sink full of dishes and my husband and children watching football. Life dragged on.

Things didn't change. They neither got better nor got worse. Bob and I stayed in the "valley" and couldn't quite make it up the hill to better times, but I was sure we would. We had been in these ruts before. It was only natural. Bob kept working ridiculous hours, and I ran around driving the girls to soccer practice, piano lessons, birthday parties, and the mall.

"Why doesn't Dad pick us up anymore?"

"Where's Dad?"

"Doesn't Dad have time for us?"

I heard it all, but I didn't have answers for any of the questions. My all-purpose reply was, "Why don't you ask him?"

I picked the girls up from Molly's restaurant once during these shaky times but didn't lay eyes on her. Would I have been able to see something in her that would have told me she was sleeping with my husband? Probably not. I trusted Bob more than he deserved.

Meanwhile, the girls continued to rave about Molly.

"She's a cool grown-up," Amy decided.

I knew I wasn't. Their mother was just the person who had given up her entire life to raise them right, and maybe I had not done so good at that.

My nest wasn't empty in the true sense, but I was in a vacant house more often than not, and it wasn't a happy place for me. I could only cook and clean so much. Soap operas didn't interest me anymore. In fact, I came to realize that I'd never developed my own set of interests, because my life revolved so much around Bob and my daughters and taking care of them. I was still a young woman but felt at least ten years older. As for my appearance, I didn't let my hair get to the point where Bob would say something about it again, but the rest of me was in a definite slump.

Since my family was resisting me to the point that I couldn't even get a compliment about a meal I slaved over, I decided that it was time to throw them a curve ball. It frightened me to change directions, but I had to do something.

"Bob, I'm going to get a part time job," I announced as he was getting undressed after a marathon day of taking care of "new customers."

"Carla, why would you want to do that?" he asked coldly, as he tossed his shirt into the laundry bin in our closet.

"I have to do something. I'm here alone all day, you don't come home, and the girls are in school. I cook, and no one eats—"

"Our kids are older now, times are changing. Just go with the flow, Carla. You don't have to do something ridiculous like that." Bob never sneered at me, but I could hear some annoyance in his voice.

"I want to get out of the house," I stated firmly.

"Who's going to drive the kids around?"

"Why don't you leave work to do it? They ask about you all the time because they don't see you anymore."

"I told you, I have new customers! And it's tax season! You know how it is, Carla!" Bob slammed into the bathroom, half undressed.

All the while he was saying this Bob was making his usual amount of money, but not anymore than he usually made, because of course he wasn't at the office. I pieced that part of the puzzle together. And he had started to miss payments on some of our bills, but I didn't know it. He kept up with everything concerning the girls but was letting everything else slide. The boats, the cars, even the mortgage. To prove how much I still trusted him, I didn't even look at the bank statements that were still coming to the house, didn't question why everything was being done "online", yet paper statements from our bank were still in the box once a month.

Bob had always done the financial business for us. Ironically, I didn't know how much money we had or even how much
the mortgage was. I was foolishly dependent on him in so many
ways. Which made his decision to leave all the more devastating.

As for me, I had caused quite a sensation by saying I was
going to get a job. The girls came to their senses, at least temporarily.

"What, Mom? How can you get a job? Who's bringing
us where we need to go?" Jenna demanded, bursting into the
kitchen while I was preparing another meal that perhaps no
one would eat, or that everyone would complain about.

"Maybe your father can find time in his busy day to accom-
modate you," I said stiffly. "Or maybe you can start appreciating
everything I do for you."

My second eldest started shuddering with emotion. "Mom,
I love you, you just don't get it," she sobbed.

That was obvious. And it would become clearer and clearer
as the weeks went on.

Molly

"SURPRISE!" I SHOOK my pom-poms as I opened the door to Bob.

He laughed. "What's this? Are you going to be a cheerleader for Halloween?" His eyes started at my new white tennis shoes, surveyed with pleasure my short red skirt, wandered over my snug white top. Then he pulled me into his chest and swung me around.

"We're having a football party tonight!" I announced.

"Wow, it doesn't get much better than that!"

Bob came over almost every night now. His clothes were starting to pile up in my bedroom, he bought food for us, and I had a constant flow of flowers. When one bouquet would start to look sad another would appear. Bob had even started to meet the girls at the restaurant. I think Becky and Jenna suspected something, but the two younger ones didn't have it figured out yet. Maybe Bob was preparing them for a change.

I was patiently waiting for the day when he would tell me he was finally leaving Carla. We had been seeing each other for a year, and he had said on more than one occasion that he was just waiting for the "right time."

That night I had tricked out the coffee table with silly party favors leftover from a Super Bowl party I had thrown the year before. The cups, napkins, and plates all had footballs and goal posts on them. Bob's favorite beer was on the table, and the game would begin in half an hour.

"I don't know if I'm going to make it through the game with you looking like that," he joked, as I handed him the bottle.

"We still have a little time before kick-off," I hinted, plopping down on his lap for a long kiss.

When we came up for air a pleased moan escaped from Bob's lips before he opened his eyes fully and said, "I want to talk to you about something before the game starts." Bob took a sip of beer and patted the couch next to him. He suddenly sounded serious, and I feared that he was going to tell me that things were over between us.

I settled in next to him with a little shiver. "What's on your mind, honey?" I asked, trying not to sound worried.

Bob took a deep breath and announced, "I'm ready to leave Carla, Molly. But I'm worried about the girls. I don't know where they fit into all this. They really like you, and I think it's going to be okay, but it's not going to be easy for them." He drew his brows together and seemed to want to go on but didn't. He gave me a questioning look.

"Bob, the girls are welcome to visit here anytime. Obviously, I don't have a lot of room, but we'll figure it out. How are you going to tell them?" I couldn't imagine how all this would play out.

"I was thinking that I'd just bring them here and we could both tell them," he replied.

"You're going to tell Carla first?" I asked.

"No, I think we should talk to the girls first, then I'll tell Carla. I want them to be ready, and to know they can be here with us if that's what they want."

Wow, I didn't expect that. Even though I knew what I was getting into by being with a man with four kids, I didn't think that Bob would expect me to open my home to the girls. He had told me their relationship with Carla was crumbling more and more as the days went by, so I probably should have expected it. But the full extent of what I was getting into didn't hit me until that night. I know I should have thought about it more, but Bob was ready to make his move and I didn't want anything to stop him. I was in love with him, and that's what really mattered. The rest of the details would fall into place as we went along. I couldn't imagine why his children would want to move into a five-room condo with us when their whole lives were in that big house in the best part of town.

"You don't think they'll tell her?" I inquired.

"No, something tells me they won't. And anyway, as soon as they know she'll know, too," he assured me.

"Make plans with them and we'll do it," I urged.

"We'll do it next Friday night. Right now, I have other things in mind." He grinned wickedly and patted his lap. I happily took my seat there again as Bob murmured, "I never knew I could be this happy."

Neither did I. But there were four road blocks suddenly in the way of my joy, and their names were Becky, Jenna, Emily, and Amy. I silently prayed that they would stay with Carla once the bomb dropped and the dust cleared, and that some kind of visitation schedule would be quickly meted out between her and Bob. That was the way it seemed to work for some of my friends who had children and had ended relations with their husbands. Until then, I would have to deal with the fallout of Bob's marriage.

"The girls and I are coming over tomorrow at six. Is that still good for you?" Bob called on Thursday morning when I was getting ready to go to the restaurant. I had one last chance to say no. I didn't take it.

"Bob, that's fine. I'll have burgers and fries ready," I promised.

"Lots of fries," he joked.

We had plans for that night. I had a bittersweet feeling that a lot was about to change for us. We would be a real couple soon and wouldn't have to hide. But that would mean revealing our secret to his family. I would have to tell my mother and friends about Bob, too. He wasn't the only one keeping our love under wraps. My stomach felt queasy thinking about what would happen when the cat was out of the bag. I'd been wanting this for a year, but the reality of it was so different than fantasizing about it. Crunch time was here.

Bob called me an hour before we were supposed to meet at my condo. I was just about to leave the restaurant and missed his call. He sounded stressed over voice mail.

"Babe, some pipes broke and leaked all over the basement. I'm sorry, I have to take care of that, because Amy's room is down there. I'll see you tomorrow, okay?"

I didn't call back. Waiting for his next call was the better option because I didn't want to add stress to the situation.

Our nights as a secret couple ended with a flood. Our life as an official couple would start with an explosion.

The Best Offense is a Great Defense

Carla

EVERY TRAGEDY HAS A silver lining, but I had a hard time finding it when Bob left me. Not only did I lose him, I lost the last bit of love my girls had for me, my home and everything in it, and my car, at least temporarily. Many of my friends in common with Bob chose him over me. Ironically, Pam, the one who tried to convince me Bob was cheating on me, was the one who stood by me, and the first friend I called.

"Carla, take a deep breath. Do you want me to come over?" she asked soothingly.

"I have to tell the girls when they come home from school. Can you be here by then?" I croaked.

"I'm on my way," Pam promised.

Why Bob would dump his indiscretions on me during his lunch hour was beyond me, but that's how he chose to do it. He even brought back the empty containers that held the shepherd's pie I had packed for him. Staring at them after the door slammed, they seemed like a metaphor for the way I suddenly felt. Every noise the house made seemed to echo and scream at me that I was alone.

No, I'm not. I'll always have my girls! I wanted to shout back.

The doorbell rang, saving me from cursing my empty home.

Pam gathered me in a hug. I couldn't even cry yet, like when someone you love suddenly dies.

"Pam, you were right. I should have listened to you!" I sobbed.

"Who is she? Did he tell you?"

"No, nothing. Just said what he had to say and left. How am I going to tell the girls?" I stressed.

"I'll be here for you. You'll get through it."

Becky and Jenna got dismissed from school a half hour before Amy and Emily. If I didn't have to pick them up for a sporting event or music lesson the two older girls walked to Amy and Emily's school to get them, then they all came home together. That was how it went that afternoon. Picking them up would have definitely been tougher. At least I'd have them all in the same place at the same time this way.

They arrived a few minutes before four o'clock. I could hear them chattering as they came up the walk, but they fell silent as soon as they entered the house. Becky and Jenna didn't react to Pam's presence, but Amy and Emily looked nervous.

"Girls, come sit down. I have to talk to you about something," I said as evenly as possible. My voice only shook a little, even though I was shell shocked.

"I made some iced tea. Can I get some for any of you?" Pam asked cheerily.

"I'm good," Becky said stubbornly, plopping down in a chair like she didn't want to be there.

"Me, too," Jenna piled on.

Emily and Amy accepted the iced tea. I waited until Pam had sat down at the table again before I started. She had to nod her encouragement before I could get any words out.

"Girls, your father left me today. He said he has another woman in his life. I want you to know that we'll get through this somehow and you don't have anything to worry about." I spoke forcefully, but I knew I was promising them things I couldn't guarantee them. Yes, we'd get through it, but we had a lot to worry about. I couldn't even start to guess what would happen next. The entire world seemed uncertain, and Bob had made it clear that he wasn't going to answer any questions willingly.

Nothing could have been as bad as the words Becky spoke then. They were even worse than Bob's.

"We know all about it, Mom. It's not news to us. Dad told us last week. We want to go live with him and Molly."

My children had known for a week that their father was leaving, and they had kept it from me?

I was so devastated that the name Becky offered didn't even register at first.

Molly.

Where had I heard that name? I saved it like an important document in my mind's computer as I watched Becky take out her cell phone, which she and I picked out together on a good mother and daughter day several weeks back, and dial her father.

"Hang up that phone, young lady. I'm your mother and you belong with me. If your father wanted you with him and Molly he would have been here to take you with him." The offending woman's name came out as a sneer, the rest as an order.

"Dad already said we could live with them. Molly is way nicer than you, Mom!" Becky was obviously the ring leader here. Jenna had been speaking out against me, too, but now she was quiet. Emily and Amy looked mortified by the entire scene. Pam looked the same.

"You're being extremely ungrateful, Becky. Your mother said to hang up the phone," Pam backed me up.

Through Becky's phone I heard the familiar drone of Bob's voicemail. "Dad, we're gonna get ready to come to Molly's. What time can you pick us up?"

Molly, Molly, Molly...

I jumped up from my seat and threw my hands up in the air. "What have I done to deserve this treatment? Someone please tell me this is just a nightmare!"

Becky clicked off her phone and yelled, "You're, like, the worst mother in the whole world! All you do is scream at us all day long and tell us we can't do what other kids do. Dad said you're having a crisis because you don't like yourself, and I believe it!" With that she turned to her sisters and said, "Let's go get ready for when Dad calls!"

Jenna gave me a long look before she followed Becky, her back stiffened. Emily and Amy were both crying now but ran out of the room with their sisters.

I clutched my pounding head as the tears came. "What is going on, Pam? How can this be happening?"

Pam lead me into the living room and made me relax on the couch.

"Bob isn't even answering his phone when he sees Becky's number. He's probably lying to them," she predicted.

I had thought that, too, because Bob was always there when one of us called.

"Pam, what do I do?" I begged.

She shook her head. "I don't know, Carla." After a short but uncomfortable silence she asked, "Who is Molly? Do we know this person? Someone at the club?"

I shrugged as several faces of younger women at the Farmingdale Golf Club, where we had memberships with our husbands, came and went before my eyes. "Maybe she's a customer at the office. Lord knows he has plenty of those," I spit.

Molly.

"You're probably right, since he's been spending so much time there."

A sudden vision came to me then. It didn't start as a face, but as a nametag. Then came the bright white starched blouse that the tag was pinned on.

"Oh, heaven's no," I gasped, holding my chest.

"Carla? Do you need an ambulance?" Pam shrieked.

"No, I know who she is. She's a goddamn waitress!" I cried.

Molly

BOB AND I HAD A WEEK of bliss in between him telling the girls about us, and him delivering the final word to his wife. We started going out in public, not hiding anymore. He seemed to have so much off his chest. I quickly fell even deeper in love with him than I already was. I loved how carefree he was, even though I knew he had a lot to think about.

"It was them I was worried about, Molly. Not her. I don't care what she thinks," he confessed to me after bringing his daughters home to their mother and returning to me.

Becky, Jenna, Emily, and Amy had run to me when he had brought them to my condo. Becky and Jenna understood what was going on right away, while Emily and Amy had needed an explanation.

"You know your dad hasn't been happy with Mom for a long time. I wanted to be with someone you girls really love, so I thought of Molly," he said sweetly, beaming from them to me.

"Dad, I'm so happy for you!" Becky acted so grown up. I knew she was fifteen, soon to be Sweet Sixteen.

Jenna looked around at my condo and said, "This is such a cool place!"

I have to confess that I didn't want them to think my place was "cool," because I didn't want them to be too comfortable there. Was I backpedaling? Probably. Originally gung-ho about accepting both Bob and his daughters, bag and baggage, now that it was really happening, I was concerned about life as I knew it slipping through my fingers. My previous choices of partners were men who had never been married nor had children. Bob was a totally new kind of guy for me. If I'd had my choice, I'd have taken him and left the girls to Carla.

But it wasn't my choice, so I would spend the time with the kids that I had to in order to stand behind Bob through his divorce. That was my limit. I'd already told Bob that I wasn't looking to be a stepmother to his children, and he was fine with that.

"But I'll support them and love them just the same," I'd added at the end, feeling guilty.

Bob had caressed my shoulders and assured me, "I totally understand. No one expects you to be a stepmother."

Imagine my surprise when, in the late afternoon after Bob left Carla and had come home from the office and right into my arms for the first time, his phone started ringing and Becky's number had come up on the screen.

We were having a romantic dinner complete with candles and mood music, and I hadn't planned on any interruptions.

"You'll call her back later, right?" I urged, when he looked worriedly at the phone on the table next to his plate.

"I don't want to wait too long in case it's something serious. No telling what Carla is going to do now," he said quietly.

I could tell how distracted he was as his phone pinged to indicate he had a message. While I was telling him about my day at the restaurant, he kept glancing at the screen. When it lit up with Jenna's number, he set down his fork and said, "I'm sorry, Molly, but I have to be sure my kids are okay." He snatched up the phone and answered it before Jenna's call went to voicemail.

I only heard one side of the conversation, but it was clear that all four of his children wanted out of that huge house Bob had put his blood, sweat, and tears into for fifteen years, and he was going to pick them up and bring them to my condo.

"It's okay, right, Molly?" he asked, after he had already promised them that he was on his way to get them.

At that point I didn't feel like I had a choice, so I said, "Sure, Bob. They can come for a few days until they're ready to go home."

Count me as the most naïve "other woman" in the world! All four girls trouped into my condo with enough clothes to last at least a week.

"Hon, can we set them up in the spare room? They have their sleeping bags," Bob said.

My heart thumped, must have missed a beat or two. I swallowed the lump in my throat and answered, "Sure, Bob."

My spare room had a treadmill in it, as well as a stationary bicycle. Those two things, which I used a few times a week, were swiftly moved to the side of the room, and pretty soon two teens and two prepubescents had their belongings scattered everywhere and I had nowhere to work out.

"This is like camping!" Emily decided.

Bob laughed. "Yeah, it's like a family camping trip, only a lot more fun!" he added.

At least that's what he thought.

That night, after the girls were all sleeping, and he and I were tucked into bed Bob held me tight against him and murmured, "Thank you for giving the girls someplace to stay."

I weighed my words carefully in reply. "I'm happy to have them here for a few days until they're comfortable going home."

The explosion came then. "Well, I stopped paying the mortgage last month, so pretty soon they aren't going to have anywhere to go home to," Bob admitted.

I was stunned into silence.

Carla

PAM CONTINUED TO BE a great friend to me. She basically moved in when the girls took their things and went off to Molly's.

"What about Jim?" I worried.

"You're more important than Jim, Carla. Especially considering I happen to know he's cheating on me again," Pam admitted softly.

"Not with Kinky Boots?" I gasped.

"No, it's someone from the golf club," she replied.

"Pam, how do you know? And how did you guess about Bob?" I wanted to know.

She chuckled, lowered her eyes. "Just my intuition."

Hers was obviously better than mine. I was starting to feel like I didn't know much, and that I was a failure at everything, including motherhood and being a good wife.

"You aren't the wrong one, Carla. Don't blame yourself. I always knew Bob was a rat."

"Pam!" I shrieked.

But we laughed, at a time when both of us clearly needed it.

Jim quickly proved to be the bigger man amongst rats, by calling Pam relentlessly for the first forty-eight hours she was with me. Meanwhile, my husband and children seemingly fell off the face of the earth. Whenever Jim would ring, I would check my screen in hopes that I would get something from one of them, anything. About the only person I heard from was our lawyer, Jack Dowd, telling me that Bob wanted a divorce, and that I could expect papers. Jack was very short with me, leaving me with the feeling that he was on Bob's side. He wouldn't even discuss the girls with me, and how I had a right to see my children, divorce or no divorce.

"He's another rat, anyway," Pam quipped.

Our little world was evidently full of rodents.

"I'm not answering the phone anymore," Pam decided stubbornly, after Jim tried too many times to coax her home.

I was envious that she had the upper hand on her cheating man, while I was a sad sack waiting for attention. When I admitted my jealousy Pam scolded gently, "You don't have to be the victim, Carla. Neither one of us do. Let's show them that we're just fine without them."

"How do we do that?" I asked, a mixture of fear and excitement bubbling up inside of me.

"First, let Bob and the girls have it the way they want it. Or at least, the way they think they want it," Pam plotted.

"You think I should let another woman steal my husband? And my children?" Pam threw me for a loop.

"No, just accept it, rather than fight about it. Maybe Bob will have his little affair for a while longer, but I'll bet the girls will get sick of being there and will want to come back to you."

Maybe Pam was right. I couldn't see any of my daughters living out of the small bags of possessions they had carried out the door.

"Okay, I'll try it," I decided.

"Meanwhile, we'll become new women, the kind of women they'll wish they never left," she replied.

"But...how?" I really didn't know anything, had a lot to learn.

"Well, I think we should start by getting jobs and learning how to be independent. Then we'll take it from there."

I remembered how I had told Bob months ago that I wanted to get a job, but my whole family had protested, because I was needed as a taxi service. Now I wished I had done it. I'd be ahead of the game.

"I'm in," I agreed.

"You sound younger already, Carla!" Pam teased.

She was right. I sounded like one of the girls! They used that line all the time.

Pam and I started to scour the classifieds online. Neither of us had ever really worked. I had raised children, Pam had been the local charity guru, always gathering the ladies of Farmingdale to pitch in to help with one good cause or another. Both in our mid-thirties, we became discouraged by what was available for job seekers with little to no experience.

"I'm certainly not going to work in a convenience store!" Pam griped.

"Or a restaurant like his new girlfriend!" I added.

"A waitress. Imagine!" Pam guffawed.

Suddenly, I saw Bob's boat being hauled down our driveway from the backyard. I jumped up from my laptop and ran for the front door. "Pam, someone is stealing the boat!" I shrieked.

"Carla, don't open the door, just look out the window and wave good-bye," my friend said calmly.

"Pam...?"

Over the next week Pam and I had more important things to think about than finding jobs. After the boat was taken away, so was my car. Then, after going out to eat, we arrived back at the house to find a lock on it that I didn't have the key for.

"I told you he was a rat," Pam murmured, trying to make the best of a bad situation.

"Where are we going now?" I cried.

"We'll go to a motel," she answered firmly. "Until you call Jack Dowd back and demand that Bob pay the mortgage."

Pam had been stopping me for days from trying to call Bob, but standing out there on the steps of my home with the clothes on my back the only belongings I had in the world now, I'd reached a breaking point. I dialed his cell. He was getting a piece of my mind whether he wanted it or not, whether it was right or wrong.

His voicemail came on, and I hung up with a curse. Then, I tried the office phone. Lara, his assistant, answered and chirped, "May I ask who's calling?"

"It's Bob's wife, Carla," I spit.

"Please hold," Lara said abruptly.

I was on hold for ten minutes. I hung up angrily, cursing, "Damn it!"

The next time I tried to use my cell it didn't work.

"He shut my phone off!" I said in disbelief.

Pam's husband Jim may have been a rat, too, but he wasn't shutting her phone off or letting things get repossessed. In fact, he was calling a very reasonable once a day now and leaving heartfelt messages, saying that he missed her, he knew he had screwed up too many times, and was there anything they could do?

"I think you should at least talk to him. He sounds sincere," I told her.

"He had seventeen years to be sincere and he couldn't figure it out," Pam said sadly.

I shook my head, grimacing. "These men, Pam! We have to show them!"

She brightened. "We will show them!" She reached for my hand, gripping it tightly.

I squeezed her fingers.

Having someone to fight back with was so gratifying. As Bob might say during a football game, "Score!"

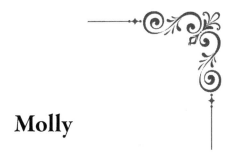

Molly

THE DOORBELL RANG AS I was hiding a shoe belonging to one of Bob's daughters. I scanned the living room one more time to see if I missed anything, before I opened the door to my mother.

"Hi Mom, how's it going?" I cried, throwing my arms around her neck. It seemed like forever since I'd seen her, and so much had happened since our last visit. We usually got together every week, but since Bob and his brood had shown up, I had missed a visit with her, much to her chagrin.

The worried furrow of her brow melted away. "I'm a lot better now that I see that you're okay," she answered.

"Oh, everything is fine. I was just a little under the weather. And way too busy." I wasn't lying. Well, not really.

I held my breath as Mom looked around my condo. "You aren't taking care of things as well as you usually do. Are you sure there isn't something you aren't telling me?"

Mothers. Pulling the wool over the eyes of mine was not easy. I wanted to fess up to everything that had been going on. But I said, "No, Mom. Nothing to report, other than I'm ready for lunch!"

"Just need the little girl's room before we go." I cringed as Mom went into the bathroom. There had to be something in there that would give everything away. Bob's pricey men's shampoo, perhaps some of his hair in the drain, a child-sized toothbrush. But Mom came out momentarily and declared herself, "Ready!"

As we left the condo I glanced at the clock. A little more than two hours until the girls got back from school. "I have an appointment later on, so I have to be home by three," I told Mom.

"You never make appointments on days we get together!" she exclaimed, and she was right. Our days together had always been sacred, and I did whatever was necessary to keep them that way. But now...

"I'm sorry, Mom. Couldn't help it today. I won't make a habit of it. I promise!"

Mom liked eating at the restaurant I worked at, loved talking to my co-workers and hearing them compliment her on raising such a hard-working and decent daughter. I couldn't take the chance that they would mention Bob, as everyone knew about him now, so I brought her for Chinese food, instead.

"So, tell me why you've been too busy to see your mother," she said, once we had a pot of jasmine tea and two small white ceramic cups in front of us with the pleasant-smelling liquid steaming up from them.

"Just the usual stuff. A lot of hours at work, and with not feeling good I've been sleeping more," I explained.

Mom nodded and unzipped her purse on the other side of the table. "Does this also have something to do with why I haven't seen you in two weeks?" A business card from Bob's accounting office was in her hand. "There was a small stack of them on the back of the toilet." Mom held eye contact with me and wouldn't back down.

Bob must have left them in the bathroom when he undressed to take a shower. Could anything have been more obvious?

My shoulders slumped. No, I couldn't fool my mom.

"Yes, that has something to do with it," I confessed.

"The town is full of rumors about this guy, Molly. The ladies told me my daughter has been running around with him and I didn't believe them. I would have much rather heard it from you."

I should have known, too, that Mom's "ladies" Bett and Margot would know all the town gossip. How quickly word got around! Bob and I had only been public for a week!

"I'm sorry, Mom. I was going to tell you in my own time, but I wanted to break it to you gently, and tell you all about him and how great he is," I moaned.

"Molly, this was a happily married man with four children! Bett and Margot said he stopped paying the mortgage and his wife and kids had to move to a motel!"

Rumors were so hurtful. I knew none of that was true, and I went on the defensive.

"Mom, don't listen to them. The girls are staying in my spare room because they don't want to be anywhere around their mother. And last thing I knew Carla was still living in the house and calling Bob nonstop at his office."

Mom's eyes widened. "You have five other people living in your condo?"

"Bob is so amazing, Mom. He's the guy for me, so yes, I'm letting his daughters stay temporarily." I know I sounded lame, but at least I wasn't lying anymore.

Mom leaned across the table and asked, dead serious, "Since when do you want to be a mother to anyone?"

I shrugged. "I don't, Mom. But I like the girls a lot and I just want to help Bob out while he's going through this tough time. He knows I don't want to be a stepmother."

She leaned back. "Molly, it isn't too often I'm disappointed in you, but I have to say I am right now."

I nodded glumly, knowing I should have told her a long time ago. Hiding my secret was a lot easier when it was just Bob coming and going. Mom had always respected my personal life and tried not to get involved, but I knew this was different.

"I understand, Mom. I can't apologize enough."

"Can you explain why you didn't tell me?" she pleaded.

"Because I knew you would try to talk me out of it, for one. But I guess the biggest reason is because I was waiting for Bob to leave his wife and I couldn't risk anyone finding out about us in the meantime."

Our pretty Chinese waitress brought our loaded plates of hot and delicious food before Mom could comment. As amazing as my lo mein smelled I had lost my appetite since ordering it. Mom didn't look all that interested in her plate, either.

"Waiting for Bob to leave his wife. I take it this little affair has been going on for quite a while?" Mom looked like she feared the answer.

"About a year," I answered.

"Oh, dear god."

The rest of the meal was tense and neither one of us could eat much, even though I had been hungry.

"You can stay and meet the girls if you want," I offered as I drove back to my condo. "They'll be getting home from school soon. That's why I couldn't stay for too long."

"I'm not so sure I'm ready for that." Mom stared out the passenger side window.

"Bob didn't have a good family life growing up, and he was never happy with Carla. He would love to meet you."

Mom just nodded.

She decided not to stay but wanted to see my spare room where the girls were "camping out." The space was definitely a mess, and I had not worked out since they took it over. Bob wanted me to join the gym where he had a membership, but I was hoping the girls would go back to Carla and I wouldn't have to.

"I hope you figure out how to put your foot down and send these kids back to their mother," Mom said tightly as she got ready to leave. She was reluctant to accept my embrace.

"Can we set an evening aside when you can come over and meet them all?" I asked hopefully.

"If that's what you want. But I'm not going to be very good company."

Mom was usually blowing me kisses over her shoulder as she left me. But not today. Today, she didn't turn back.

I couldn't turn back, either.

Carla

PAM AND I STAYED IN a local motel for three nights until Bob started paying the mortgage on the house again. The lock came off and we were able to go back. What a relief, even though everything there reminded me of him.

Bob also had my phone turned back on, and I soon found out the motive.

"Mom, we're coming over for more clothes," Becky called on Sunday afternoon to tell me.

"That's fine," was all I would offer, though I missed my daughters so much.

Bob pulled up in his silver Infinity and the four girls popped out of it and ran up the sidewalk. He soon had his cell phone up to his ear, no doubt talking to the Homewrecker. As expected, Becky and Jenna were business-like, but my two youngest girls looked around longingly before they came to hug me. All four of them looked wrinkled, like four fish out of water.

"Are you guys getting your clothes?" Becky tried to motivate Emily and Amy, who weren't moving too fast. "Dad is waiting for us, and you know he wants to be watching the game."

Emily and Amy decided to follow their older sisters.

"Chinks in the armor already," Pam pointed out once they were in their rooms. "The fantasy is crumbling."

I shook my head, biting my lip so I wouldn't cry. "I don't know how much longer I can do this, Pam."

I had promised Pam that, even though I had every right to see my children until Bob and I decided custody in court, I would not rock the boat. Instead, I would let the girls come back to me. Now that I was in the house again, I felt that things were looking up for them to return, and not just for another bag of clothes.

Emily came out of her room first and rejoined Pam and I at the table to wait for her sisters.

"Molly must have a pretty nice place if you don't want to be here with your Mom," Pam commented, putting a glass of lemonade down in front of her.

I knew what Pam was doing.

"Becky thinks Molly's condo is cool, but I don't think so. There isn't enough room for all of us there," Emily mumbled, focusing on the drink.

"Molly lives in a condo?" I was in disbelief but tried not to sound it.

"Yeah, and we're all staying in the same room," my second youngest admitted.

"Dad and his girlfriend are in a different room?" Pam asked.

Emily rolled her eyes. "Of course. But there's only two bedrooms, and we're stuck in the other one all together. With our sleeping bags! But Dad and Molly are going to get some beds for us."

Although I was heartbroken for my daughters, I had to swallow my emotions for the time being.

Our conversation came to an abrupt halt when Becky returned to the kitchen. She was rolling a suitcase Bob and I had bought her for our cruise the previous summer.

"Where's Jenna and Amy?" she demanded.

Emily shrugged and drank down her lemonade. I sensed a deep reluctance in her to comply with Becky's wishes. Meanwhile, Becky left her case in the middle of the floor and started yelling to Jenna and Amy.

"Dad is waiting for us! We have to go! Molly is cooking, and we don't want to be late!" Becky passed a look at me, presumably to see what my reaction would be. I felt my face turning red, I was so upset, but Pam winked at me in an attempt to keep me calm.

Becky soon had the troops rounded up, and that's exactly how they looked as they marched in a line out the door back to Bob's car. I summoned every bit of strength I had inside me to keep from running after them and demanding to know why he was doing this to our family. Once they were gone, I met up with Pam in the living room, where she had turned on, of all things, a football game.

"Oh Pam, turn that off. It reminds me too much of Bob," I scolded, but I couldn't help but chuckle.

"I kind of like watching," she admitted.

"How about a glass of wine?" I asked. "And I'll get some cheese, too."

"Sounds like a plan," she agreed.

As I was preparing the wine and cheese I was listening to the familiar play-by-play of the game in the next room. My hands stopped moving and I let my mind drift away from reality. For a few precious moments the past was the present, and it wasn't Pam on the couch, but Bob and our beautiful girls, and we were still a happy and complete family without Molly in the way. I shook my head to bring myself back to the here and now. Pretending was never my strong suit.

I arranged the carefully sliced cheese on a glass plate and with the bottle of red wine and two goblets I pushed through the swinging door to the living room.

"First down and ten on the twenty-seven yard line," came the announcer's voice, one I had heard a thousand times. "Hand off to Peters, and he gains four, before he's stopped. Time out called. When we come back, we'll have a second down and six on the—"

I nearly dropped the whole tray. Everything clanked when I set it down on the coffee table.

"Carla, are you okay? You look like you've just seen a ghost!" Pam rose from the couch and put her hand gently on my shoulder to steady me.

I could hardly hear Pam even though she was right next to me. My mind was on the move again, but this time with simple subtraction. Ten yards minus four yards was six. First down and ten. Second down and six. It was simple!

"Pam, I get it! I understand!"

"What do you understand?" she asked.

"Football! I understand now! Bob tried to teach me all these years about what a down is, and I never quite got it. But I just figured it out!" I made myself comfortable on the couch and poured us generous glasses of wine.

The next play further confirmed my new knowledge. The running back gained three more yards, so it was third down and three! Pam had to help me out a little with simple explanations of the punting and the field goal kicking, but now that I had figured out the basics myself, I started to get interested in the game.

Sitting on the couch, drinking wine, watching football. I'd done it all so many times over the years. This time it was special. I felt like I had overcome something that made me less attractive in Bob's eyes. Perhaps it was silly of me to make such a big deal out of my little victory, because I still had such a long way to go. But I had to take what I could get.

My transformation had begun.

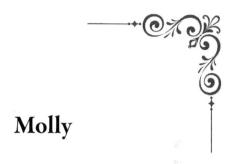

Molly

THE NIGHT I INVITED my mother over to meet Bob and the girls went well enough, but I could tell she wasn't happy, and she didn't exactly come willingly. Bob poured on the charm, but my mom wasn't one to be talked into liking anyone she didn't want to like. And she made it clear that she didn't want to like Bob, though she cut the girls some slack, referring to them as "innocent bystanders."

"Mom, Bob's ex-wife is really making things hard on them, that's why they don't want to be with her," I tried to explain the next time I saw her, which was three days after the dinner I served at my condo.

"Molly, she's not his ex-wife yet, and remember, you'll never change the fact that she's the mother of his children and he loved her enough to be married to her for fifteen years," Mom fought.

Leave it to mothers to point out the obvious things that make your heart skip beats.

"They were eighteen when they got married, and she was already pregnant! He didn't have a choice." Even I knew I was digging myself a hole, but I wanted Mom to support me in what I was doing. She always did. But this time, she was making things damn tough!

71

"If you're in love the way you say you are, I have to live with it. But I don't like it," she said firmly.

"He really is wonderful," I tried to convince her for the millionth time already.

"There are plenty of single men without children who are wonderful, too," she replied stiffly.

"Mom, you know my history with men. Bob isn't like any of them!"

"He certainly isn't!"

I guess I said the wrong thing and walked into that comment, but I still had not heard the worst.

"Mom—"

"Just remember, if he did it to her, he'll do it to you."

Mom made it clear that the discussion was over. She was visibly shaken. Maybe she was thinking about how Dad had divorced her after twenty-five years of marriage and moved to an undisclosed location. She had always presumed he had left the area because he had met someone new, but we had never found out for sure. Dad had been gone for over a decade. We had not heard anything from him, not a single letter or phone call.

Bob was nothing like him. I was sure of that. He was a great father. If he wasn't, he would send the girls back to his wife where they were supposed to be. Instead, he protected them from her.

By this time Bob and his daughters had been with me for six full weeks, in which they hardly saw Carla. Though things were going a lot differently than I had planned I felt like I was doing the right thing for the girls by letting them stay with us and trying to give them good advice.

Still, the times I looked forward to most were when Bob would sneak home for an extended lunch period and we were able to have a couple of hours to ourselves. I lived for those moments and had changed my work times, so we could have those precious rendezvous. Bob continued to promise that Becky, Jenna, Emily, and Amy would be going home to their mother whether they wanted to or not, while the terms of the divorce and custody were ironed out, but that had not happened yet. In fact, they were moving into my condo more and more every week. Bob and I had gone shopping for four single beds that would fit in my spare room, and we had moved my gym equipment down to a storage unit in the basement.

"I think we should buy a house together," he said, after we had set up the beds, which filled up the room and left hardly any space for walking, as small as they were.

We had never discussed such a big step. My palms started to sweat. "Really?" I asked.

"Really. The girls love being with you and it sure would be great if they were more comfortable."

I wasn't so sure that all the girls were completely in love with being in my condo, or that they accepted Bob and I as a couple. They had definitely thought of the whole situation as an adventure at first, but I could see the wear and tear of the disruption of their lives starting to affect the two youngest girls, especially Emily. She was the most emotional one of the four, and sometimes had nothing to say to any of us, even when Bob tried to pull her out of her sour moods.

"Have you mentioned that to them?" I asked.

"They were the ones that asked me about it. They want to live in a house with us."

The thought occurred to me that perhaps Bob was going to try to get full custody of them without telling me, though I knew well enough that a father rarely pulled that off unless the mother was unfit. Bob had horror stories about nasty phone calls from Carla and told me how she ran out of the house to yell at him whenever he dropped the girls off to pick up clothes or other belongings, but I doubted that made her an unfit mother.

"Aren't they going to be with Carla most of the time once things are settled?" I inquired carefully.

"They don't want to be with her! You hear how they talk about her!" Bob cried.

Becky and Jenna were the ones that bad-mouthed their mother the most, I think, and Amy and Emily followed along to please their sisters and father. Even though Bob said that Carla was behaving badly at every turn I still didn't want them to say things against her. After all, she was their mother. Maybe I was sensitive, too, being that my own mother and I were in a bit of a relationship slump.

"Yes, Bob. I do. And it's not good."

"You're the best, Molly. Carla should be thankful that you're trying to make the girls think nicely about her," Bob gushed.

"She just gives us these sad looks whenever we go over there to bring more stuff here!" Jenna griped.

"Ugh, I can't stand those looks of hers!" Becky piled on.

If I'd had any sense, I would have scolded Bob for letting them disrespect their mother like that, or maybe I would have noticed that the girls and Bob said two different things about Carla. None of Bob's daughters ever said that Carla was running down the sidewalk and chasing Bob's car like he insisted. I believed him, and maybe they did, too.

I lost my mind those hours that Bob and I were together without anyone else in the way. He was the best lover I'd ever had. Never would I have thought that I would be one of those women who lost all common sense over physical love, but suddenly I was. I couldn't get enough of him. Nothing else seemed to matter. I thought about him and those moments of passion no matter where I was and who I was with, itching and praying to get back to him. I was willing to do whatever I had to do to keep him.

I was in deep.

Carla

PAM AND I WERE BOTH pretty good bakers, so we got this crazy idea, after several weeks of scanning the employment websites, to put an ad in the local paper. We would tell the world that we would bake cakes, pies, cookies, cupcakes, and many other delights, for any occasion.

"I'll bet we won't get a single call," Pam mused, as we admired our box ad on the second page of the Farmingdale Gazette. We checked the online version, too.

The next day we got our first request to bake a large order of cupcakes for a local basketball team. While we were hard at work on the two hundred goodies Pam's cell rang again with an order for a wedding cake.

"My baker is in the hospital and I need the cake for the day after tomorrow! I'll pay any price for it!" The mother of the bride was frantic on the other end of the phone.

Pam calmed her down and we agreed on a price for the triple-layer cake.

"You ladies are saints!" the woman cried.

"Would you be willing to hand some business cards out at the wedding?" Pam asked.

I shrugged at her questioningly and she winked back.

We didn't have business cards!

"I'll stand on a street corner and hand them out to everyone if you can get this cake baked for me!" Mrs. Casey promised.

We baked cupcakes all day. The next day, we pulled off the cake. And the phone rang a few more times with advance orders for Christmas, which was quickly approaching. In between, we went to the local copy center and had simple cards printed. We were suddenly business women, and no one was more surprised than us. Except for my daughters.

"What's all this stuff?" Becky had not taken so much interest in anything I did since she became a rude teenager and started treating me like a second-class citizen. She scanned the kitchen counter, which had baking utensils and supplies all over it. Meanwhile, she was pulling her suitcase around while her father waited in his car, which had a noticeable dent in the passenger side door.

"We have a little bit of a baking business going," I answered, only wanting to reveal enough to make her and the rest of my family curious.

"You have, like, a job? And you're making money?" My eldest looked at me like it was the single most preposterous thing she had ever heard.

"Yes, Becky. We're doing pretty good. Would you like a brownie?" Pam spoke up.

"No thanks. Dad is waiting!" Becky huffed, but she looked intrigued. Teenagers weren't very good at hiding their true emotions.

Pam winked at me. Lately, we had a lot to wink about.

The sudden success of the baking business was not the only change in our lives.

"I don't think this room should be going to waste," Pam suggested, as we surveyed Bob's small fitness room, which was connected to the master bedroom.

We started to work out on Mondays, Wednesday, and Fridays, after we finished baking and making deliveries for the day. Hearing from Jenna that she and her sisters were occupying the room in Molly's condo where she used to have her workout equipment inspired me to step just a little harder on the stair-climbing machine and run just a little faster on the treadmill.

After a month in business we also treated ourselves to a massage therapy session at the local beauty salon, where we had always had our hair done. While we were there, I made a dramatic decision to cut several inches off my hair and to color it back to its original chestnut brown. The woman that looked back at me in the mirror pleased and scared me at the same time. I wasn't that dreary person that Bob had left in the lurch for sparkly-eyed Molly. And I was quickly becoming a woman who wouldn't have someone's feet wiped on her like a welcome mat. We even left business cards at the salon and handed a few out to interested acquaintances.

"Who could guess all these things would happen to us?" Pam marveled over lunch.

"Certainly not me!" I replied, wide-eyed as we clinked wine glasses.

Things were about to get even more interesting.

Emily, suitcase next to her, was waiting on the back steps of the house when we arrived home.

As her mother, my first reaction was outrage at myself. Had I missed her call? Glancing at my phone screen before I got out of Pam's car, I saw I had missed nothing. Emily stood up and rushed over as soon as she saw us pull in front of the garage.

She almost knocked me over, she came at me so hard.

"Mommy, I want to come home!" she sobbed.

As I rumpled her golden blond hair, I gave Pam a long look. She smiled back softly.

"I'll be in the house." As Pam went in the back door she brought in Emily's things.

"Did something happen at Molly's?" I asked, just to be sure.

"No, I just don't like it there! I miss my room and our house, but most of all I miss you."

From the mouths of babes!

"Come on, let's go and put your stuff away. Your father dropped you off?" We walked hand in hand to the house.

"No, I had Stephanie's mom bring me. I didn't want to ask Dad because he would have tried to talk me out of it," Emily explained.

Is that what Bob was trying to do?

"You'll have to call him, so he knows you're okay," I told her.

I felt her hand stiffen in mine. "Can you call him?"

I didn't care to call Bob, but I relented. First, I helped Emily get her room back together while Pam baked a small order of croissants for a customer.

My eleven-year-old, who would be having a birthday soon, complimented me on my fresh new look. "You're so pretty!" she gushed.

Was I? I waved my hand at her in dismissal. "Don't be silly. You all got your father's good looks!" I teased.

"Really, Mommy. You look amazing."

Whatever happiness Emily and I shared was quickly brushed under the rug when I called Bob about her location.

"Let me talk to her. She never once said she wanted to be with you. What are you saying to her?" Bob demanded.

"I'm not saying anything to her or to any of the girls. Why are you making them feel guilty about wanting to come home?"

Bob hung up on me, but moments later Emily's phone rang. From the kitchen Pam and I could hear Bob trying to control Emily. She was having none of it.

"I don't want you telling Molly bad things about Mommy anymore!" she cried.

After Bob was done talking to her, she was in a lot of distress. Pam and I brought her back around with a piece of warm peach pie with cool cream on top.

"Daddy says bad things to his new girlfriend about me?" I inquired tentatively.

"Yeah, and Molly tells us to talk nice about you," Emily offered.

I swallowed hard, my mouth suddenly dry because I had to acknowledge that Molly the Homewrecker had done something to defend me.

"She does?"

"Molly is really nice," Emily insisted.

I couldn't imagine that I would ever think a woman who stole husbands and daughters was "nice." But I supposed it was good of her to not allow my children to say bad things against me.

That night, when I went to say goodnight to Emily she whispered, "I miss Becky and Jenna and Amy."

I was trying to be strong, but that did it. "I do, too," I admitted, tears quickly coming to the surface.

"Mommy, Amy wants to come home. But she's scared and doesn't want to make Dad and Becky mad."

I pressed my lips together as I thought of what I could say to make Emily feel better.

"Why don't we give her a call in the morning and tell her we miss her and want her to come home?" I suggested.

"That sounds good," Emily agreed.

I hardly slept at all that night, wishing my youngest girl was tucked into her own bed.

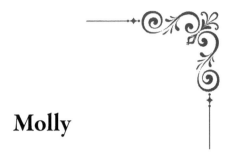

Molly

ALREADY ON EDGE AFTER a car accident that dented his prize Infinity, Bob was devastated when Emily went home to Carla without even telling us.

"Damn Carla is messing with her mind!" he assured me.

As for Becky, her concern was completely self-centered. "Can we move her bed out of here now that she's gone so we'll have more room for us?" she demanded. Bob jumped right to it and took Emily's bed apart. We brought it downstairs to my storage area where my gym equipment was starting to get dusty.

More than anyone, Becky was starting to grate on my last nerve. She was rude and ungrateful for everything we did for her. If there was anyone I wanted to leave, it was her.

"She's going through so much, and she knows that she's going to have to eventually go home to Carla." Bob explained it away with excuses. For the life of me, I couldn't figure out why Carla wasn't demanding that they go home. Maybe she was an unfit mother! Up to that point I'd had no contact with Carla whatsoever. But that was about to change.

The day after Emily went home Becky and Jenna reported to Bob and me that Amy had been talking to Carla on her cell phone right after breakfast.

"Mom was trying to talk her into going home," Becky blabbed. "Amy was bawling."

The two older girls were going to the mall with friends that day, while Bob and I took Amy to a local football game. She was very quiet on the way and seemed down. Halfway there I looked over the back seat of Bob's Infinity and she was asleep.

"Carla must be putting stress on her," Bob said quietly.

"The poor kid," I murmured. Of all the girls Amy was my favorite. She was a sweet and well-mannered kid, unlike Becky, and to a lesser extent, Jenna.

"Believe me, when Carla gets going there's hell to pay."

"Why would she want to do that to her own child?" I wondered aloud.

"You don't know Carla," was Bob's best answer.

Amy blinked her filmy eyes when we got to Farmingdale Field and dragged herself out of the car.

"You okay, kid?" Bob asked gently.

"Yeah, Daddy. Just tired," Amy said with a sigh.

As we were taking our seats in the small stadium, I felt my phone vibrate in my purse. I didn't recognize the number but answered it anyway in case it was some emergency with my mom.

"Hello?"

Carla was on the other end calling me a homewrecker, amongst other things. Bob heard her voice and hissed, "How the hell did she get your number? Hang up on her!"

I happily obliged, but I was definitely shaken by her words.

Amy was shivering between us, looking guilty. She confessed to giving Carla my number "in case of an emergency."

I put my arm around her and assured her that it wasn't her fault. She didn't hug me back.

Later that evening Bob and I talked about looking at houses again.

"I think it's time. Emily probably only went back because she wanted to have her own room again," he said.

"We'll start looking," I agreed.

That week we spent some time online together and came up with three houses in the area that we liked. They had three bedrooms, still not big enough so that each of the girls could have their own rooms, but better than my condo. The prices made me gulp. How could we afford anything that expensive with Bob getting a divorce and giving half of everything he had to Carla, if not more?

"Well, you'll have money from the sale of the condo, right? You said you had some equity built up?" he asked.

"Yes, but it still means a much bigger mortgage payment, and I don't want to be going to work just to pay bills. I want some quality of life, too, Bob," I insisted.

"Hey, don't worry! We'll still have plenty of fun," he teased.

I nodded listlessly. It had been a long and emotionally charged day. The following day was even worse.

I had the day off and was at the condo to welcome Amy home from school. The two older girls were staying after for a school play rehearsal. They both had minor roles, but Becky seemed to think it was her big break toward becoming a celebrity. I was happy they were at school and that Amy and I would have some girl time.

Amy had other things in mind.

"Molly, I want to go home, but I don't want Daddy to yell at me," she confided in me.

My heart sank. Bob was going to be upset.

"Is your mom pressuring you to come home? Becky and Jenna said you talked to her on the phone yesterday and—"

Amy shook her head, fear on her pretty, young face. "No, Molly. It's my own decision to go home. I miss my room and Emily, but most of all I miss my mom."

I nodded, swallowing hard. "I'll talk to your dad and make sure he understands why you want to go home."

"Molly, Mom didn't call and yell at you because she was mad at you. She called to yell at you because she was mad at Dad for trying to keep me here, and he never answers the phone when she calls." Amy stared at me, waiting for my reaction.

How could a nine-year-old kid know this?

"Well, I'm sure she doesn't like me very much, either," I said softly.

"I want Mom to like you, because I like you even if I want to go home. Will you meet Mom when I go home?"

The kid seemed to have more sense than the three adults fighting over her.

"We'll see," was all I could promise.

Amy would hold me to my word.

"Amy is a child, and she's being pressured." Bob exploded when I told him about Amy's request to go home, after she was in bed and snoring.

"Bob, she insisted that the decision is all hers." I had a headache by now, and it was starting to seem to me that Bob thought he was having some big competition with Carla, with the prizes being their kids.

"Oh, hell, Molly, this just gets worse all the time. Carla is going to get everything I worked so hard for all these years, and in the end, she's going to get the kids, too!" Bob buried his face in his hands and clutched his forehead. I leaned my cheek against his shoulder and rubbed his back.

I didn't have the heart to tell him that Amy wanted me to meet Carla. My hope was that she would simply forget about such rubbish. Instead, I murmured, "Bob, we'll have each other. Remember that."

"I can't wait until all this is over, so we can build our life together without that witch in the way!" he spit.

That made two of us. In my wildest nightmares I couldn't have imagined how hard all this would be.

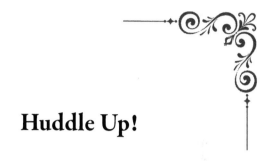

Huddle Up!

Carla

ONE BY ONE, MY GIRLS came back to me, all on their own. After Emily it was Amy, but only after she finally convinced Bob that it was her choice. Then Jenna a month later, and finally, Becky. My eldest told me Bob had warned them they would be "forced" to return once we went to court. They made their own decisions long before that happened. I'd be lying if I claimed that I wasn't pleased, but what made me happier was that they were satisfied to pick up their lives as they had known them before Bob left.

"Dad is turning into such a jerk, Mom. I like Molly better than him," Becky sniffed, the night we were eating dinner together for the first time in months. "I don't even want to visit him anymore, but I'll go to see Molly."

"Molly is the one that always told us to be nice to you, even when Dad was being mean," Jenna added.

I had heard that one several times, but still didn't want to believe it.

"Mommy, I still wish you would meet her," Amy cried.

Amy had been asking me for months now to meet this woman who, rumor had it, had a fat engagement ring from Bob before our divorce was even final, and was planning to buy a house with him so that the girls would have a bigger place to visit. Bob seemed to want to keep us from meeting, and he handled all the pick-ups and drop-offs when custody was settled. Doors were thrown open, doors were slammed closed. I only saw him through car and house windows.

"I will someday," I murmured, since it was inevitable.

The girls volunteered a lot of information, and I said as little about it as I could.

"Keep taking the high road," Pam reminded me when necessary.

I knew Bob had a lot to say about me, and most of it wasn't nice. In fact, some of the things he told the girls and his new woman were downright lies. About the only thing I did that I regretted was calling Molly that day on her cell phone when Amy wanted to come home and Bob was stretching out the process, trying to make our youngest feel guilty. The need to protect my child had trumped common sense, and since Bob wouldn't take my calls I decided to haul off on Molly. I heard loud and clear when Bob told her to hang up on me, and I carried around that impression of her.

Meanwhile, my life continued to change as much as Bob's. In some ways, even more.

Pam had decided to go back to her husband Jim, so it was me and the girls living in the house. My great friend still spent a lot of time with us, since our baking business was booming. My kitchen was usually the scene of our activity, though sometimes we switched to hers. The girls loved being a part of the business, and proved to be very helpful at packaging goodies. Sometimes they took part in the deliveries, too.

"Dad thinks your business is a joke," Becky was sure to tell us. "But I told him it's for real and he got mad."

Leave it to Becky to make her voice heard!

Financially, I was getting a generous amount of money from the divorce, as well as the house, which was nearly paid in full, since Bob had put extra money toward the mortgage over the years since we first moved in. How ironic that his foresight into paying the house off early wouldn't come to fruition until he had destroyed the very family he built the place for. With the money Pam and I made from our business added to what I was getting from the settlement, the girls and I were very comfortable.

Rather than driving the car that was returned to me after Bob started paying the monthly payment again, I traded it in for an SUV that was more comfortable for the five of us. We could take it on road trips, and it would fit all our suitcases and sports equipment. We had our first trip planned for the summer after Bob left me for Molly. I couldn't help but remember that he had first laid eyes on her soon before we would take a family cruise.

"So much has changed since then, Carla. You've turned your life around, and you're a new and better person. Let it go and be happy. Maybe this was all meant to be," Pam soothed.

Maybe she was right.

I could have never dreamed that I would look in the mirror and see a person staring back at me that had lost thirty pounds, had beautiful, thick hair, and wore youthful clothes. Sometimes, men even stared at me, which took some getting used to. I wasn't ready for anyone in my life again, but it didn't mean I wasn't enjoying the attention. Carla was fully out of Bob's shadow now, and even though I had lost a lot of friends when he'd left I had kept some, too. True friends stuck around, and I wasn't interested in the others.

The excitement of summer vacation was upon us. The girls only had a week left of school, then we would be hitting the interstates to visit my parents in Georgia before continuing on to Florida and all the theme parks. Later, we would hit the Gulf Coast for fun in the sun before returning to Farmingdale. Pam would run the business the three weeks we were gone, and one of our old friends would fill in for me. With so many things to look forward to, and life being so new and exciting, I shouldn't have felt so edgy.

"Everything is going to be fine while you're gone," Pam assured me.

But it wasn't that.

"Pam, there's something I have to do before we leave. Both for the girls and for me," I said softly. "And I need your support."

"Whatever you want, Carla. You know I'll be there for you."

Pam didn't ask what I was getting at, but looked at me expectantly.

"I need to meet Molly and let Bob go forever," I blurted.

Pam's face softened. "I think that's a great idea, Carla."

"And I need to do it for the girls, too." They had asked me so many times to meet her.

"Yes, it's time."

My plan was to go to the scene of the original crime, namely, the restaurant that Molly still worked at. We would have dinner to celebrate the end of the school year, and I would be cordial to Molly.

"Let's not tell the girls. We'll pick them up from school and go to dinner. It'll be a surprise," I plotted.

A big surprise. For all involved.

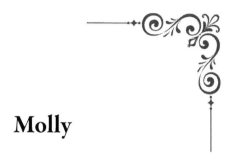

Molly

CARLA ISN'T LYING WHEN she said it was Bob who tried to keep us from meeting each other. The girls wanted it, because they loved us both. But Bob was so damn mad that they had all moved out of my condo before the terms of the divorce and custody were settled legally that he wanted to do anything to strike back at Carla, even if it was through the children. Even if it was through me. I couldn't admit to myself that all this was happening, what with Mom putting the continued pressure on me to find a man without so many problems, and with my body screaming with pleasure whenever Bob and I had time alone.

With summer vacation on the near horizon, we had three full weeks without the kids to look forward to, while Carla took them on a road trip. Bob even made that a controversy.

"Carla can hardly find her way to the supermarket. And she thinks she's driving to Florida?" he sneered.

Let them go! was my secret thought. Bob was taking vacation time, too, and we were planning some day trips. I coveted the ten days we would have together. I smiled weakly at his comment, but even I thought it was unnecessary, and probably even untrue.

Now when the girls came over to be with Bob at the court-appointed times we heard all about what was going on at home in glowing terms. Bob always had comments about whatever Carla was supposedly doing, and oftentimes he didn't wait until he was out of earshot of his daughters. I didn't think it was my place to butt in, but once in a while his comeback was so bad that I had to say something to him later.

"Bob, maybe you shouldn't have said that in front of them," I told him after one particularly awful insult.

"Molly, they're my children and I'll say whatever I want in front of them! Don't you think Carla is doing the same thing?"

Truth be told, I didn't. And even if she was, two wrongs didn't make it right.

Carla certainly didn't sound like the woman I had met in the restaurant when she and Bob were still together. Becky especially, who at one time was a bigger critic of her mother than even Bob was, lauded Carla's accomplishments. Not only did Carla have a successful baking business, but she looked great and, most annoying to Bob, she watched football now.

"Mom understands everything, and we watch every Sunday and Monday," Jenna bragged, during the football season.

Bob just rolled his eyes at that one, but I could see he was holding a lot in.

"I tried to teach Carla about football for almost twenty years and it didn't work. They're lying!" he boomed later, like we were talking about some life-threatening disease.

He was in a bad mood for a week after that.

On the next to last day of the school year Bob picked the girls up and we had a little celebration at my condo before they left on their trip with Carla. We were still living there, as I had made several excuses why I wasn't ready to buy a house with Bob. He was still pushing for it. I couldn't tell him that Mom was on the verge of disowning me already, and had I buckled to the pressure of buying the house it would have likely been the last nail in my coffin with her. Still, that afternoon Bob was making promises to the girls that we had not discussed beforehand.

"Molly and me are hoping to be buying a house by the time you get back from your vacation," Bob boasted.

He had the idea in his head that the four girls would want to spend more time with us if they had more room, while I was pretty sure they were content with things just the way they were, as was I.

"Oh, that's cool, Dad," Becky said offhandedly.

They continued to chatter happily about their upcoming trip. I thought that would be the last time I would see them before they left.

I was wrong.

"Party of six just came in," our new hostess announced a couple of hours into my shift the next day.

"Hope they're good tippers," I joked casually, though it almost wasn't a joke, when I thought of Bob's insistence the previous evening after he brought the girls home that we needed to get serious about getting out of my condo.

I tried to forget the conversation as I headed toward the dining room. As I entered the doors to the room an older couple who came in often distracted me as I was gathering up menus, asking me for soda refills. When I turned to the round table in the middle of the room, I suddenly pulled up short and sucked in my breath.

"Hi Molly!" Amy sang, waving both her hands at me. Her three sisters were chirping out their own greetings. Two women who didn't look at all familiar to me were at the table with them. Was one of them Carla?

I was caught. To turn around would have been awkward but forcing myself to step closer was just as strange. I swallowed hard and decided to suck it up.

"Happy summer vacation." I wanted desperately to sound casual, but my voice was shaking.

As I passed out the menus and recited the specials of the week, I met eyes briefly with the attractive woman between Emily and Jenna, and recognized her as Carla, though a much shinier model than the one I had seen the first time. I had memorized my spiel after having said it numerous times that week, but it came out stilted. I was so nervous I felt like I had just started waitressing that day.

"Thank you," Carla said, when I handed her a menu.

I took their drink orders and scurried away to the bar. While I waited for the bartender to get me their sodas, Tanya, the waitress who had been the first person to take note of Bob's apparent interest in me, appeared next to me with her own drink order.

"Molly, are you okay? You look like you just saw a ghost," she commented.

I could have asked her to take the table for me.

Instead, I answered, "Yes, I'm fine. Just tired." Then, I told myself, *this is your chance to make things easier for everyone.*

My choice was to finish the job I had started.

Carla

SHE WAS TENSE, I COULD tell. From the table I could see her talking to another waitress while she was getting our drinks, and I fully expected that she wouldn't come back.

"When she brings our soda do you want me to do it?" Becky conspired, leaning into me so no one else could hear.

"Yes." While we were on our way to the table, I had asked Becky to introduce us. Molly had been so abrupt while she passed out menus and rattled off the specials in a quivery voice that the opportunity for Becky to act on my wish had not come yet.

To my surprise Molly came back. I saw her hands shaking as she passed out our sodas. Becky, never one to be afraid to speak, cleared her throat and said, "Molly, this is my mom Carla and her friend Pam."

Molly tentatively met my eyes and raised her hand to give me a little wave.

I bravely reached out to her for a handshake. Her palm was sweating when it met mine.

"Nice to finally meet you, Molly. I've heard a lot of great things about you." It was a ridiculous line after all we had been through, and yet it was accurate in its own way. I hoped I didn't sound sarcastic, because that's not what I wanted.

"You, too, Carla," she said tightly. She wasn't any more comfortable with Pam.

I got a good look at Molly. She certainly was attractive, but she looked tired. Not quite the carefree woman Bob, me, and my daughters had met. Maybe she was just having a bad day. Then again, perhaps it was more than that.

Molly acted professionally through the entire meal, and of course there were extra fries for the girls. Amy was especially happy that I had finally broken the ice with Molly.

"Mommy, I'm so proud of you," she gushed. It wasn't the only time she had said that. Everything was so different now not only between Amy and me, but with all the girls. We had been through some rough times but had truly come full circle.

"Me, too," Pam said, smiling at me from across the table.

But I wanted more.

After we ordered dessert, I saw Molly sit down at a two-seater table near a window and take her apron off. She put an adding machine and stacks of receipts in front of her.

"Excuse me for a minute," I said without explanation, and walked across the dining room to approach Molly's table.

She looked up from her work when I was within a few steps, and a look of fear passed over her pretty face.

"I'm sorry to disturb you. Can we talk for a few minutes?" I asked.

"Umm, sure," she said quickly, and moved her work closer to give me space.

"I see you're busy. You don't have to move anything for me." I pulled out the chair on the other side of the table and made myself comfortable.

"Oh, no problem." She met my eyes. Inside hers I saw a nice person, and I forgave her, right then and there. I had to remember that Bob and I had been having problems, and she just happened to be there, and Bob acted on it. But I couldn't say that to her. I had to keep it simple.

"Molly, I'm giving you and Bob my blessing. For the girls, I think we all should have better communication, because I want them to continue to have a good relationship with him."

Molly's face softened, and she nodded. "I agree, Carla. It's really hard when you're both saying bad things about each other. I'm an adult and I can handle it, but I worry about the girls. I love them all and want the best for them."

I believed that. But she had something just a little bit wrong.

"Molly, I don't bash Bob. Are the girls telling you I am?"

"Oh no, Carla. They only say nice things about you now. Maybe in the beginning they were, but not in a long time."

"So, Bob is telling you I'm being a witch?" I chuckled, and she joined me, her shoulders relaxing.

"He's said a few things," was all she could offer, her eyes on the table now.

"Well, it's not true. Maybe at the beginning, like you said, but not in a long time."

She nodded. "I understand."

"Would you be willing to exchange cell phone numbers, so we can keep in touch about the girls?"

"Carla, that would be great," she agreed.

"And I won't use it for any other reason," I promised, alluding to the day I called her phone and told her she was a homewrecker, something I was still ashamed of. If there was one thing I would have liked to erase, it was that.

She gave me her number and I typed it into my phone, then I gave her mine. What followed was an uncomfortable moment in which I seemed stuck to the chair. I wanted to say more, to defend myself from whatever Bob may have been saying against me, but I erred on the side of caution. Going any further could have turned a pleasant and fruitful chat into something completely different. I stood up to go.

"Carla, thanks for coming over, and for bringing the girls. I hope you have an amazing trip," Molly said, her confidence seeming to surge.

"You're welcome on all counts and thank you for the well-wishes. I think it's going to be a great experience for all of us." Our eyes met one last time, then our hands did. This time her palm wasn't sweaty, and her handshake was as firm as mine.

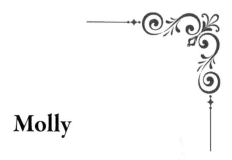

Molly

"WHAT'S THE MATTER, baby?" Bob crooned that night, after I had met Carla in the restaurant.

"Nothing, babe. Just tired," I lied, when the truth was that meeting her left more questions than answers, and the questions were driving me mad to the point that I didn't even want the usual physical thrills that Bob provided.

"Well, let's get a good night's sleep so we can feel good looking at the houses tomorrow."

Bob was really pushing hard about buying a house. I continued to make weak protests and needed to step them up.

Meanwhile, I worried, too. Would the girls tell him about the dinner? Would they make a liar out of me? Time would tell. I wished that I had spoken up to Carla the way I wanted to. "Carla, let's keep this between you and me because it's only going to start problems when Bob finds out." That was all that I had to say. But then maybe she would have known that things were not as rosy as they were supposed to be.

"Molly?" Bob was trying to get a reply out of me, while all these things were running through my mind.

Now was the time to let my true feelings be known. Bob didn't have nearly as much money as he used to have now that he had to give so much to Carla and the girls, something that he complained about a lot more than I did. He was counting on the equity I had built up in my condo to help fund this house that I didn't even want. I liked having the equity and had worked hard for it. Things often turned out different than expected, but it sure seemed like I would get the bad end of the stick if I buckled to his pressure.

"Bob, I don't really want to look at those houses tomorrow. Can we do something fun instead?"

His vacation was starting, Carla and the girls were leaving, and I had taken the time off from the restaurant to enjoy it. Why spend it doing something I didn't even want to do?

Bob sat up in bed and narrowed his eyes at me. "We've been talking about this for months and now you tell me that you don't want to buy a house?" he sneered.

Bob was usually easy-going, but I was starting to see this side of him more and more and I didn't like it.

"I didn't want you to be upset," I admitted.

He rolled out of bed. "Well, I am upset. I spent a hell of a lot of time looking for the perfect place for us and now I feel like I wasted it. I don't like wasting time, Molly."

I knew that. Bob was high energy and was always on the go. In fact, I would call him a "Type A" personality. That certainly wasn't me. I liked to be busy, but I wasn't obsessive about it, and I liked to work hard for the reward of having a good time.

Bob left the room. Before long I heard a sports show blasting on the enormous flat screened TV he had bought earlier in the year to watch the football playoffs.

We rarely had disagreements, but when we did it was usually me running to him to straighten things out. This time I stood my ground and continued to lie in bed and think about all my problems. Bob came back to bed during the night after I had fallen asleep. We slept back to back for the first time in our young relationship.

Bob struck back at me by going to his golf club and hanging out with his buddies for almost half of his vacation. We went on a couple of day trips, to the beach and to a spa in the nearby mountains, but there was a definite tension between us. I wondered if he was still working off my lack of desire to look at houses, or if one of the girls had told him about the restaurant visit. While his ex and their children were on the road, he made several phone calls to them demanding to know where they were and if they were all right, after originally scoffing at the notion of Carla taking them on the adventure.

"Daddy, we're fine! We're at Sea World and it's so awesome. Mom is doing great with driving and—" grimacing, Bob pressed the off button on his phone, thus cutting off the conversation that he had started with his youngest daughter.

A sick feeling roiled in my stomach.

"Carla had better bring them back safely! What was she thinking, driving all that way!"

I heard from each of the girls at least once, telling me that they were having their best vacation ever. If they called while I was with Bob, I would dial them back when he was away, so I didn't have to hear his negative comments. Before long I realized that I was hiding more from him than I was telling him. But I didn't feel guilty, because our time in the bedroom, the one thing that was keeping Bob and I going, suddenly wasn't enough.

Mom and I had never talked about matters of intimacy, but she guessed from hints I had made that much of my willingness to take Bob, even with all the problems he brought with him, had a lot to do with our sex life. I wouldn't soon forget her warning on the subject.

"Molly, just remember there has to be more to a relationship than that."

With all my other boyfriends there was always more than that.

Bob was a master puppeteer in that department. But I was becoming more and more resistant to having my strings pulled.

Then, he really tugged the wrong one.

Our much-anticipated vacation was a major disappointment, and soon I was walking back into the restaurant and lying to my friends and co-workers about how great it was. I expected that I would have to force myself to return, but I wasn't walking on air the way I thought I would be, and I was happy to be back.

Tanya saw through my façade. "Everything okay?" she whispered when we were both picking up orders.

I gave her a false smile, my voice tinged with irony. "Sure, Tanya. Everything is great." "Let me know if you need someone to talk to," she said eagerly.

I definitely needed someone to talk to, and it would eventually be Tanya. But someone came before her.

I called my mother on my lunch break. "Mom? Want to have lunch at the restaurant before my shift tomorrow?"

"Sure, hon. What time?" she asked.

"How about one thirty?"

"See you then." Mom sounded confused, even though we used to have before-my-shift get togethers all the time. They had all but dried up since Bob and his problems had taken over my life.

That night, after closing the restaurant early because of a very slow night, I got home and found Bob stretched out on the couch talking on his cell phone and watching baseball. He didn't immediately hear me come in, as the television was on loud and the front door was behind the couch.

"Hey," I said softly.

Bob had his wallet on the arm of the couch with a business card on top of it. He abruptly ended his conversation, shoving the card in his wallet.

"Hey, you're early," he replied, then stood to cuddle me the way he always had. His breath smelled like beer and I could tell he was a little drunk. Not that we didn't drink, because we did, but we usually did it together. I thought it was strange that he had emptied a few beers without me. The evidence was on the coffee table in front of him.

"The place was totally dead, so we shut down," I explained, talking over the game, which I found annoying. I glanced toward the screen.

Bob got the hint and dove for the remote control to turn the volume down. He seemed to be nervous about something. I didn't trust him.

Bob trusted me a little too much.

I sat down to unwind and watch the game with him. He got me a beer and we made small talk. My eyes kept drifting toward his wallet, which he left on the end table. I saw the edge of the business card, which just happened to be pink. Who would have a pink business card?

I waited patiently until Bob went to the bathroom. Then, I carefully grabbed the wallet and pulled out the card. *Call me!* was written in a feminine, loopy script. The card was from an instructor at a local yoga studio. Ironically, we had gone to one of her classes a few months before, but Bob had quickly decided that he "didn't care for" the class and we never went back. Now I knew why.

By the time Bob appeared again, the card was back in the wallet and the wallet back on the table just as he left it.

If he did it to her, he'll do it to you. Mom's words echoed in my head.

How did mothers know everything?

Carla

NEVER IN MY LIFE WOULD I have thought that I could get behind the wheel of my SUV and drive five thousand miles. Bob would have never let me do that when we were married. He used to plan everything. At the time I felt like he was "taking care of me." After the road trip with the girls I realized that in many ways he really wasn't; he had been holding me back from being independent, from being a complete person.

"Pam, he was strangling me, and I didn't even know it!" I cried.

I was on the back patio of the house that my ex-husband built, with my best friend, drinking wine. The girls were unpacked and tucked into their rooms, safe and sound, after the fun and exhaustion of the road. Though I was still and always would be the responsible parent, I could let my hair down a little more now that we were home and I didn't have to drive long distances with the girls in tow.

"I told you I thought he was a rat!" Pam lightened the moment, and I took the bait.

"Sounds like you knew my husband better than I did." I shook my head, chuckling.

Silence fell around us. My shoulders relaxed, and I breathed in the night air, enjoying the sound of the crickets making their summer chirps in the grass. A pair of fireflies were getting closer to us. I had not seen fireflies in years.

"Business was good while you were gone, and we have several orders to fill in the next week," Pam said softly.

"Oh Pam, this is all so hard to believe." I felt so peaceful, yet so accomplished, too.

"You worked hard for it, Carla," she reminded me.

"We worked hard," I corrected her.

"No, I'm not just talking about our business. I'm talking about everything you've done since Bob left. You played your cards so well. You have a lot to be proud of."

Another thing I never had a chance to do when Bob was around: be proud. He usually took the credit for everything, even if I had something to do with it. Like raising the girls. I remembered how he would always make it sound like he was the one doing everything for them, and I would let him get away with it. I let him get away with a lot. Part of me still wanted to. It's hard to teach an old dog new tricks.

"It's tough for me to think like that, Pam," I admitted, feeling squeamish.

"You're still a work in progress."

I nodded.

Bob had kept after me throughout nearly the entire trip. Now, the phone was strangely quiet.

"I figured he'd be calling and making sure I brought the kids back in one piece," I said bitterly.

"He probably finally figured out he was making a fool of himself," Pam pointed out.

Even after everything Bob had put me through, I was worried as to why he suddenly disappeared. I even thought about calling Molly to be sure all was normal, but Pam talked me out of it.

"I'm sure you'll hear from him when he wants something," she quipped.

As usual, Pam was right. But in my wildest musings I couldn't guess what Bob would want the next time I saw him.

Pam and I were baking a large order of sweets when the doorbell rang five days later. The girls were in the pool with a few of their friends, the sliding glass door from the kitchen thrown open so we could keep tabs on them.

"What timing. I hope it's important!" I griped, licking yellow frosting off my knuckle rather than let it go to waste, before putting down my decorating tube and quickly washing my hands.

"Are the girls expecting someone else?" Pam asked.

I shrugged. "I didn't think so. But are teenagers ever expecting anyone else?" I joked, wiping my hands dry on my apron.

At the front door, I peeked out the peephole, before scurrying back to the kitchen, my heart racing. "Pam, Bob's at the door! Can you answer it?"

Pam dropped her mixing spoon and rinsed her hands. "Be happy to. Did he tell you he was coming?"

"No, but one of the girls could have forgotten to tell me." I followed Pam to the door but stood where Bob couldn't see me when she opened it.

"Hi, Pam. Is Carla around?" Bob sounded a lot different than he had over the phone the last time I'd talked to him. He wasn't yelling or being insulting anymore. In fact, his voice had a lilt of innocence, like a child who had gotten into trouble and was trying to worm his way back into the good graces of his mother.

Taking a deep breath for strength, I decided to step into the picture before Pam could answer him. Pam took the cue and went back into the kitchen, but I knew that if I needed her she would be there for me, as she had all along.

I had not been able to see Bob well through the peephole, so I wasn't prepared for the man that was standing in front of me. Bob had always been impeccably dressed and just as nicely coiffed when we were married. He had let himself go in some regards. Still a handsome man by any stretch of the imagination, Bob was much more casual than he used to be. Wearing baggy shorts and a Hawaiian shirt, his sneakers were dirty, he had a five o'clock shadow, and his hair was overdue for a cut. When he smiled at me, something he had not done for at least a year, he came across as fake.

Had he appeared on the doorstep sooner I might have been sucked back under his spell, but it had been a long time now and we had just been through too much to go backward. I asked him, "What can I do for you, Bob? Did you want to see the girls?"

If I had to find a word to describe the way he looked, I would choose "vulnerable." He certainly wasn't the cocky, in-control man who had walked out on me without warning.

"No, Carla. I wanted to see you," he answered.

Perhaps I'm a cold person, but I felt nothing for him either way, and though I sensed he was looking for an invitation I wouldn't let him in the door. He peered over my shoulder curiously, even though I tried to block his view.

"What do you want?" I didn't know what to say to him or how to say it but was aware I sounded harsh.

"Listen, can I stay in the guest room for a few days?" he said, like it was a perfectly natural request.

I felt my face heat up. "What on earth are you talking about, Bob?"

"Molly and I had a fight and I don't want to go back to her place right now. Do you mind if—"

"Yes, I mind very much. How could you even think I'd let you stay here? You haven't had a nice word to say to me for months, and you tried to turn my children away from me."

Bob still didn't come to the door when he picked the girls up, just pulled up in front of the house and waited for them, like when they had all decided to move into Molly's condo after he left me.

"Carla, that was Molly saying all those things about you. Didn't the girls tell you that?"

I couldn't believe my ears. Bob was proving himself to be a bigger rat.

"Actually, Bob, the girls have nicer things to say about your new girlfriend than they ever have to say about you. And come to think of it, when I talked to her at the restaurant on the last day of school, I thought she was pretty nice, too." The words just came out naturally, even though I had told the girls not to tell him Molly and I had met, and especially not to tell him we had exchanged phone numbers. Maybe Molly had told him?

Bob pulled back as if I had bitten him. "What the hell are you talking about?"

Evidently, she had not.

"I wanted to meet your girlfriend and make peace with her, so I took the girls to her restaurant before we left for our vacation." I felt so confident. The tables were completely turned.

"Carla, you're a liar. The girls didn't tell me that and neither did Molly," Bob fought.

"Did you still want to stay in the spare room?"

"Carla, why are you such a damn witch? And why the hell do you have to lie?" Bob was stomping down the front walk back to his car. He jumped in and left rubber on the pavement as he pulled away from the curb.

After slamming the door, I gathered my thoughts to decide my next move.

I knew what to do. Where was my phone?

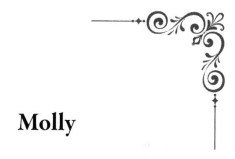

Molly

EVEN THOUGH I HAD FOUND the pink business card and had caught Bob red-handed I didn't want to believe what was really going on. Maybe we had not bought a house together, but I had still invested a great deal into my relationship with him and it was hard to let it go. Inevitably, I compared my situation with Bob to Mom's with Dad. Mom had tried everything to hold things together with Dad. None of it had worked, but not for wont of trying.

I was also embarrassed that I had let myself get into such a bind. The day after I found the incriminating card, Mom and I went to lunch as planned, and although I hinted at some problems with Bob I didn't tell her everything. But my disgust grew for a week, while Bob tiptoed around me and continued to call Carla and the girls during the final days of their trip. He was a total jerk to all of them. That seemed to be his only initiative, because when he knew they would be back he didn't make any plan to see them.

"This is the first and last time she's going to endanger my children like that!" he scoffed after he hung up on her. "They'll be home after three."

"So, you'll stop and see them and make sure they're still in one piece?" I asked, a sarcastic edge to my voice.

113

"We'll have them over in a few days. I have too much to do at the office tonight."

The signs were all there. Long days and nights at the office, phone calls that suddenly ended when I entered the room, little interest in our sex life anymore.

After he left, I called Mom. It was put up or shut up time.

"Mom, I have some stuff to tell you," I started tentatively, shook up from Bob's attitude as well as his huffy exit.

"Tell me you've finally learned your lesson!" she quipped hopefully.

"Come over?" I asked.

"Be there soon."

A full confessional followed.

"You're a grown woman and I'm not in the business of saying 'I told you so.' But I'm going to tell you to end it now, Molly. Don't let it go any further."

"I have something else to tell you," I murmured.

Mom stared at me. "Please don't tell me you're pregnant."

I had to laugh. "Heaven forbid, Mom! I'm smarter than that!"

Mom lifted her brows at me, and I realized the irony of my words. Maybe I wasn't so smart.

"I have a secret I've been keeping from Bob, and it's about time I tell him when I kick him out."

My next confession was about seeing Carla and the girls in the restaurant.

"She's actually really nice, Mom. Bob was lying to me about her."

"She sounds reasonable and decent," Mom agreed.

"Yes. I have not talked to her since then, and I guess that after Bob is gone I won't be able to see the girls anymore, but it was good that we cleared up the conflict." Though I tried to stop them, some light tears came to my eyes when I thought of not seeing Bob's daughters again. At that point I liked them a lot more than him. We'd been through some tough times, but I couldn't really blame them. They were kids, and they had had their lives torn apart. One of their parents was a louse. The cards had been stacked against them. But they had all survived, and Carla had, too.

As for me, I still had work to do to get my life back to where I wanted it to be.

Bob didn't get home until ten that night. He had been drinking but tried to hide it.

"Drinking at the office, Bob?" I sneered.

"Just one. I have to do something to get me through the pile of paperwork on my desk."

He wasn't even that good of a liar. I'd seen better.

"Bob, I know you haven't been at the office." I wanted him to disappear, and I wanted it fast. No beating around the bush.

He started to unbutton his shirt. "What are you talking about, Molly? Where else would I be?" He was still in his work clothes, but they were very rumpled, like they had been in a pile on someone's floor. In fact, he was struggling with a button, and upon closer inspection, his shirt was done up crooked. In his haste to leave the yoga instructor to come home to me, he had screwed up.

"Maybe you were doing yoga?" I inquired. Then, "Do me a favor, Bob. Don't take your clothes off again. You've done it too many times today already. Go back to her. Go anywhere. I don't want you here anymore!" I strode over to the closet we shared and pulled out several of his shirts that were on hangers.

"I have no idea what you're talking about!" was his weak defense. "You sound just like Carla now."

Bob gave me the perfect opportunity to spill my secret about meeting Carla, but I was so bent on getting him out of my condo that I missed it.

"Get out! If you don't leave, I'm calling the police. Go to Miss Yoga and move in with her!" I continued to pull his clothes out of my closet and throw them on the bed.

"You're a homewrecker just like Carla said you are! You ruined my life with her, now you're ruining our life together!" Bob cried.

It was the last thing he said. As he moved some of his clothes and personal effects into his car, he shot me hurt looks, as if I was going to feel bad for him, but didn't say anything more. I sat on the couch, that we had shared so many times, with my arms folded stubbornly, until he finally left. Once he was gone, I spent several hours getting the rest of his things together, so he wouldn't have to stay long when he came back. By the time I fell into bed, exhausted but happily alone, it was three in the morning.

The following day I was working the night shift at the restaurant. Shortly before I left my cell rang, and Carla's name came up.

Interesting.

Carla

"HI, MOLLY. I HOPE YOU don't mind me calling you, but I have to warn you about something," I began.

"No problem, Carla, but I'm going to be leaving for work soon, so I might have to drive and talk," she said pleasantly.

"Okay, well, Bob just left my house. He asked me if he could stay here and said that you threw him out."

A short silence ensued before Molly croaked, "Bob wanted to stay with you? After all the crap he said about you?"

I chuckled. "Yes, he looked pretty desperate." I wanted to ask her what my ex-husband had done to make her toss him out, but I wasn't sure it was my place to get too friendly with Molly. As it turned out, she was more than willing to share.

"I found a business card in his wallet last week from a yoga studio. He's been cheating on me!"

A blush heated up my cheeks. Bob was cheating on the woman that wrecked our family. Cheating on the cheater. Maybe at an earlier date I would have gloated about his behavior, but now I was just disgusted.

"Molly, I'm really sorry," I offered instead.

"Well, I guess I deserve it," Molly murmured.

"No woman deserves that, Molly," I assured her.

"Thanks, Carla. That really means a lot to me coming from you. You certainly have no reason to treat me fairly, and yet you have."

"You've treated my girls really well. It must not have been easy, having them in your condo." Just as when I talked to her in the restaurant, I really liked this woman, and now that Bob had cheated on her, too, I felt a deeper connection to her.

"It wasn't, but I'm glad I did it. I'll miss them."

From Molly's end of the connection I heard a loud banging. Bob had to be back at her condo.

"Is that him?" I asked excitedly.

"Yes, his car is out front. I'd better deal with him or else I'm going to be late for my shift."

"Molly, one other thing. I let it slip that you and I talked that day in the restaurant. I apologize, I thought you would have told him," I said quickly, before she could get away.

The banging was getting louder. I hoped she would be okay.

"That's fine, Carla. He needed to know anyway. Listen, I have to go before he breaks my door down. Thanks for calling." Molly sounded harried before she clicked the phone off.

For a few minutes I sat alone, quietly, listening to the sounds of the girls and their friends out in the pool, and Pam in the kitchen baking. Had I done the right thing? There was little doubt in my mind that I had.

"Everything okay, partner?" Pam was in the kitchen doorway.

"Yes, fine," I answered.

I told her the entire saga that had taken place in the past half hour. Hard to believe that such a short amount of time had passed.

"You know what I realize, Pam?" I said thoughtfully.

"I'm listening," Pam said.

"Bob was looking for someone, anyone, so he could get away from me. Molly just happened to be there. Wrong place, wrong time."

Pam nodded. "I think you're right about that, Carla."

"If it wasn't her, it would have been someone else. She's a victim, too." I only used the word "victim" to prove my point. Molly and I were too strong to be victims in the true sense.

"You like Molly, don't you?" Pam guessed.

"I know I'm not supposed to, but I do," I admitted.

Pam tapped her index finger against her lips, then snapped her fingers.

"Carla, I just had an idea," she ventured.

"I can see that," I joked. "Do tell."

"Well, didn't we talk about partnering up with someone who knows about food prep and catering and growing our business that way, too?"

We had done that, but, "I don't see the connection, Pam."

"Molly's in the food service industry. She probably has some knowledge of catering."

I grinned. "Don't you think I'm in enough hot water already without bringing Molly on as a business partner?"

"Or, you could continue to not care what Bob thinks and do what you need to do to build our business," Pam hinted.

I nodded and told her, "Let me think about it."

And I would. But in my mind, Molly had to make the next phone call. I couldn't pursue any kind of relationship with her if she just wanted to fade into the background. I had to honor her feelings.

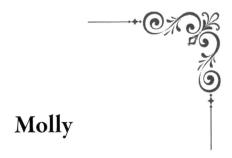

Molly

WHAT I SAID TO CARLA was no lie. I thought he would break down the door. Not only was he banging on it with his fists, he was kicking it, too.

"Open the damn door, Molly. We need to talk," Bob screeched.

I wasn't afraid of him when I swung it open to face him.

"Get the rest of your stuff and get the hell out of here," I hissed, pointing to the pile of boxes I'd made in the living room.

"Is that all you have to say to me after you kept an important bit of information from me?" he barked.

I laughed in his face. "Oh, because you're so great cheating on me with a yoga instructor? Take a good, long look at yourself, Bob, before you point your finger at me."

He ignored me and went on with his own tirade. "You saw my ex-wife in the restaurant and talked to her and you didn't even tell me about it?"

"Honestly, I didn't think it was any of your business. She was nice to me, I was nice to her, we came to an understanding, and that was that. Meanwhile, you continued to trash her, so you wouldn't have believed anything I said, anyway." I probably should have told him, but with the secrets he was keeping from me, it hardly seemed like a big deal now.

"You aren't any better than her. Two witches. Two homewreckers. All you women are alike." Leave it to Bob to make himself out to be the innocent one, even while he bounced from woman to woman.

"Are you going to tell that to the yoga instructor, too?" I spit.

"I don't know what you're talking about," Bob sniffed.

He picked up his boxes and moved himself out of my condo, out of my life.

As relieved as I was, my home had an uncomfortable silence and emptiness to it once he slammed the door for the last time. I was glad I had to go to work. So much had happened in the past hour. I had lived a whole lifetime in it. Yet I was still, somehow, on time for my shift.

To keep busy, I took on extra hours at the restaurant for the next month. In my free time, which was more limited than usual, I saw Mom and put my life as a single woman back on track. My spare room became my mini gym again, and I disappeared every trace of Bob from my condo.

To my delight, the girls continued to come in the restaurant with their friends. They were so beautiful and well mannered now that their lives had become normal again. They didn't mention Bob, other than to tell me that they saw him on a regular basis.

"Dad is okay," is the way Becky, still the spokesperson, put it.

Shortly after Bob left me, Tanya, my friend at the restaurant, told me of a rumor that was going around town.

"The whole world is talking about how he's living in a motel room and running around with the married yoga lady!"

So, the real homewrecker was Bob, not me, and evidently, he had found himself another witch.

The other bit of news I heard was that with all his shenanigans, Bob's business was going down the drain. He was digging his own hole.

As for his other two witches, we met again one early evening in the fall when Carla picked the girls up from the restaurant. They were back in school already.

"Nice to see you again, Molly," she said, smiling pleasantly.

She looked pretty and happy.

"You, too, Carla," I replied.

"Listen, I have a proposition for you. Something my business partner and I have been throwing around for a month or two."

A business proposition? For me?

I was all ears as she told me how her and her baking partner Pam wanted to start catering weddings and other social functions but needed someone who knew the food service industry better than they did.

"Wow, that sounds interesting." Carla didn't know that she had hit a nerve. I'd always wanted to be in business for myself. I liked my job, but I had a degree in culinary arts and had always thought I could do better.

"Think about it and let me know," Carla said, before she left with the girls.

I pondered it for a couple of days, and the more I did, the more excited I got. I had to call her back, afraid they would find someone else and I would miss my chance. I talked to Mom about it, too.

"If you think it would work out given your history with Carla, then you should go for it. It sounds like a great opportunity," was Mom's way of giving me her blessing.

I called Carla.

"I'd love to work with you and Pam," I gushed. "My only concern is that I'm single and have to keep my job until I start making money."

"I totally understand that, Molly. I didn't expect that you would be able to commit your whole life to it," Carla replied.

"I'll commit what I can, and the better it goes the more time I can put into it."

She and I made plans to meet. Pam would also be present, and the three of us would hash out a business plan.

"Molly, thanks for calling back. I think this is going to work out great." Carla's tone was happy.

"Me, too, Carla. I can't wait to start," I assured her.

The Witch

MOLLY PROVED TO BE a great addition to our baking business. Because Pam and I were already known around town it was easier to expand into catering, and into surrounding towns and cities. At first Molly and I kept our relationship a business one, but we honestly liked each other, and of course the girls loved her, so it was only natural that we would become personal friends.

Bob had not been faithful to either one of us, but he was true to our daughters. He was on time when he picked them up, and even came to the door now. We could speak a few words in greeting or exchange information about the kids.

Bob would often be looking over my shoulder into the house, or would ask innocent-sounding questions like, "How's business going?" I knew he was dying to find out how Molly and I were getting along, but I wasn't interested in telling him. I'm sure the girls did their share of blabbing about our friendship, and I didn't tell them not to. Nor did I ask Bob anything personal, though I knew from Pam and other friends that he was drinking and womanizing and had lost many of our mutual contacts. His business wasn't what it used to be, either. Not all customers wanted to deal with an accountant who acted so unprofessionally outside the office.

Perhaps the funniest thing I heard was that Bob was trying to get a men's football team together in town. And guess who was going to be quarterback?

But I didn't pass judgement. I wish Bob the best.

Proving that I'm not such a witch after all.

The Homewrecker

IF SOMEONE HAD TRIED to tell me that Carla and I would become close friends as well as business partners after her husband left her for me, I would have never believed them. Life sure works in mysterious ways. That we both came out as winners proves that.

Even better, Carla helped to make one of my biggest dreams come true. Within a year of starting the catering end of the business I would be able to leave the restaurant and put all my effort into expanding our reach outside of Farmingdale. Weddings, baby showers, birthday bashes, anniversaries. Carla, Pam, and I were the go-to trio for every occasion.

We even did a certain Superbowl party that a very familiar man just happened to be at. He was drunk and happily making his way from one young woman to another, not even realizing that we were there and observing the whole charade.

Bob.

"Once a rat, always a rat," Pam joked. I knew all about how Pam had long ago called Bob out.

We all giggled.

Carla reached for my hand. "Narrow escape for both of us, Molly," she murmured, gently squeezing my fingers.

I pulled my hand out of hers and held it up between us. "High five!" I cried.

"High five!" she replied with a grin.

Touchdown!

Dear Reader,

For eight years I've been writing and publishing true-to-life stories for a group of well-known women's magazines. Aware of my success, my writer friends have encouraged me to publish similar tales in book form. My "Women Like Us" series came to life from their encouragement.

Although Carla and Molly are fictitious characters, their struggles are our struggles. They're women faced with making choices that will have lasting impact on their lives. They're women with the courage to face conflict head on, the strength to move forward, and the resolve to carry on. Carla and Molly are women like you. Women like me. Women like us.

I hope you enjoy Book Three of my series!

Happy Reading!

Brenda K. Stone

Contact Information

IF YOU ENJOYED *Two Sides to Every Story,* please help other readers find this book:

1. Write a review: http://www.amazon.com
2. Write a review: http://www.goodreads.com
3. Follow me on Facebook: https://www.facebook.com/bkstoneauthor
4. Follow me on Twitter: https://twitter.com/bkstoneauthor
5. Follow me on Instagram: https://instagram.com//bkstoneauthor
6. Visit my website at http://www.brendakstone.com and sign up for my free newsletter

Also by

Brenda K. Stone:

Girls of Glam Rock Series
Girls Gone Groupie
Gunning for Groupie Gold
Live Vicariously Through Me
Women Like Us Series
Transformations
Tangled Webs

COMING MARCH 2019

Families Matter
Women Like Us, Book 4
Five stories about families in crisis, including

Sisters Are Forever:

EDDIE WAS MARY'S FIRST serious boyfriend. She was a late bloomer of sorts, partly because she was a serious student in high school and didn't want her quest to go to a good college interrupted. But it was anyway, when Eddie moved to our town and started attending our school midway through her senior year. I had just started ninth grade in the same school, Danielle was a sophomore, and Kitty was a junior, so we saw the whole thing unfold.

Eddie came to Crawford High from California, a golden boy surfing into our dull Midwestern town on a curling wave of blue, the same color as his sparkling eyes. Mary, who never seemed to be interested in any guy even though she was pretty and certainly had her chances, changed overnight when she first laid eyes on Eddie.

I remember being at the dinner table the evening after the school day that had brought the new guy to our school. Mary could hardly eat anything, and Mary loved to eat whatever simple but delicious dish Mom would invent for us on our shoe-string budget.

"Honey, are you sick?" Mom had asked.

Looking past us all and out the window, Mary had said, "Yes, love sick."

None of us had ever heard her say such a thing. When I think now of how she had gazed through that pane of glass at the road, it was like she suddenly wanted to get on any piece of pavement that would take her to Eddie Kay. And it didn't take her long to find that piece of pavement.

About the Author

Brenda K. Stone is the pen name for Barb Lee, a native of Western Massachusetts who loves to write, travel the world, hike the world, and go to rock concerts. When not engaging in these particular adventures or the several other activities she enjoys that leave her no time for rest, you can find her "doing research" with her nose in a rock and roll biography and her black bunny Gert not far away, probably sleeping.

Read more at https://brendakstone.com/.

Made in the USA
Middletown, DE
09 March 2019